A DRIFTER'S PRIDE

They found Giff Dixon outside of town, lying beside his dead horse, half dead himself, with a belly full of buckshot.

They needed a crooked job done, a job that was too tough for their crew of gunslingers. So they gave him his choice—he could take their job or crawl back into the desert and die.

Dixon took it. But he turned on the land grabbers with all the power and vengeance of a strong man, with nothing left to fight for but his pride . . .

PLAY A LONE HAND

Bantam Books by Luke Short
Ask your bookseller for the books you have missed

PLAY A LONE HAND
LUKE SHORT

PLAY A LONE HAND
A Bantam Book

PRINTING HISTORY
Houghton Mifflin edition published September 1951

Serialized in COLLIER'S MAGAZINE
November, December 1950

Bantam edition / January 1953
2nd printing .... January 1953
New Bantam edition / September 1958
4th printing .... October 1958
5th printing .... February 1969
New Bantam edition / May 1974
7th printing .... July 1974
8th printing .... July 1981

ISBN 0–553–13751–4

Published simultaneously in the United States and Canada

Bantam Books are published by Bantam Books, Inc. Its trademark, consisting of the words "Bantam Books" and the por-
trayal of a bantam, is Registered in U.S. Patent and Trademark
Office and in other countries. Marca Registrada. Bantam
Books, Inc., 666 Fifth Avenue, New York, New York 10103.

PRINTED IN THE UNITED STATES OF AMERICA

17 16 15 14 13 12 11 10 9 8

1

FOR THE second morning in succession Cass Murray stood in the rear doorway of his livery and watched the young man washing up at the water trough by the corral.

This obsession with cleanliness brought no judgment from Cass: he knew a hayloft was no sort of bed, and it was only plain comfort that pushed a man into shaking the chaff out of his shirt and washing the dust from his body after a night there. It was the man's modesty that troubled him.

His back to the livery, the young man was washing his upper body in a furtive and hurried way, almost as if he were in a panic to get back into his shirt before he was observed.

Suddenly, as if sensing he was being watched in the bright early morning sunlight, he looked over his shoulder and saw Cass regarding him. The taciturn pride and defiance on his dark face as he quickly buttoned his soiled calico shirt brought a moment of embarrassment to Cass, who turned and tramped up the runway toward the office.

Cass unlocked the office, crossed it to the battered roll-top desk next to the dirty front window and was rummaging around a drawer for the key to the grain bin when he heard the footsteps in the runway. Cass was a middle-aged man and not easily put out of countenance, but when he heard the footsteps pause at the door, he felt a strange reluctance to look up.

"Did you count them?" a voice asked dryly.

Cass turned his pleasantly heavy face to the door,

frowned, and saw the young man watching him. "Count what?"

"The buckshot holes in my belly. That's what you wanted to see, wasn't it?"

The young man was tall, long-jawed and badly in need of a shave. There was an implacable reserve in his dark eyes that were smoky with resentment now. Cass placidly gathered up a handful of matches, crossed the office and extended them to the young man. This overnight forfeit of matches was the only price Cass ever exacted for a night's lodging in the hayloft.

The young man accepted them and put them in his shirt pocket. Cass noticed then that the sack of tobacco which had been in the shirt pocket the day before was not there now. That fact combined with the memory of the young man's pride made Cass's voice oddly gentle as he asked, "Had breakfast?"

"I've got to see a man."

"Give him time to get up," Cass said mildly. "As soon as I've bought you breakfast I want to talk to you, Dixon."

A faint surprise at being called by name was reflected in Dixon's face; he only nodded, his expression one of wariness as Cass shouldered past him into the runway, and waited on the plankwalk for Dixon to join him.

Corazon was just stirring. The low sun was bright on the serrated row of wind-scoured storefronts opposite. A swamper at the Plains Bar across the street appropriated a barrel from the stack in front of the saloon and was standing on it to wash windows at this improbable hour. Above and beyond the stores on Grant Street the cedar-stippled foothills of the mountains seemed to rise out of the very edge of town, their distance deceptive in the clear light flooding from the plains to the east. The smell of cool dust was everywhere.

At the Family Cafe downstreet, they turned in and took counter stools. Since Cass was paying for Dixon's breakfast he ordered it, making it a big one, and watched Dixon wolf it down in famished silence.

When they were both finished, Cass extended his sack of tobacco to the younger man. After they had both fashioned cigarettes and Dixon had lighted Cass's, he rose abruptly. "I'm much obliged for the breakfast. I'll go back now and give your hostler a hand."

Cass looked at him obliquely. "I thought you had to see a man."

"I can do that later."

"You can help the hostler later, too. Sit down."

Dixon sat down again. He stared at his empty coffee cup, his face contained, still wary, expecting nothing and wanting nothing.

"Found work?" Cass asked him.

He received a brief, sardonic and wondering glance from Dixon, along with a negative shake of the head.

"How do you figure to, coming in here the way you did?"

Without bothering to glance at him, Dixon put his hands on the counter, as if to rise.

"Hell, I'm not scolding you," Cass said shortly. "I want to know."

Dixon's voice was toneless. "I'd like to know, too."

"For three weeks now, I've been waiting for Sheriff Edwards to get the word to pick you up. So has everybody else. That's why you can't get a riding job. That's why you couldn't get one even it you hadn't sold your saddle to pay Doc Miller." He paused. *"Are* you going to be picked up?"

"I don't think so."

"Then don't be so damn touchy about the holes in your belly. The whole town knows they're there."

Dixon said nothing; he was rigidly watching his empty coffee cup, as if bare politeness demanded that he listen in patience to the man who had bought him breakfast.

Cass had his moment of doubt, then. Dixon was a broke stranger, prideful and secretive, but any man who'd been found beside a dead horse, half-alive and with a belly full of buckshot, had earned the right to his silences. Cass remembered the day a month ago when the pair of trail drivers delivered Dixon; he was lying in their chuck wagon because he was too hurt to ride. The Texas trail hands were in a hurry to get back with their wagon, and all they could tell the sheriff was that a stampede had scattered their herd all over Beaver County and that in rounding it up one of their riders had come across Dixon. He wasn't at a camp, but at the edge of some brakes. His horse had been ridden to death and he was near death. Here he was and here his saddle was, they said, and drove off.

Doc Miller had pried the buckshot out of him, and Mrs. Miller had nursed and fed him. Three days ago, they had turned him loose, and his first act had been to sell his saddle to Burton for enough money to settle Doc's bill for treatment, nursing and board.

Two days of fruitless hunting for work, two nights in the livery hayloft brought his history up to date, Cass thought without much enthusiasm. *But he paid Doc,* Cass remembered. *I guess I'll do it.*

He reached in the hip pocket of his farmer's bib overalls and brought out a tattered envelope which he flipped on the counter.

"Sheriff Edwards got that a couple weeks ago. He turned it over to me and I forgot it until last night. It's from the General Land Office. There's a special agent coming out here along with his surveyor. They want Edwards to dig up a couple of horses and a pack mule —also a combination guide, cook, packer and chainman. Want the job?"

Dixon reached out and picked up the envelope, but he did not read the letter inside. He put the envelope down gently and said in a flat voice, "I would if I had the horses and knew the country."

"I got the horses and they'll have maps of the country," Cass said impatiently. "The job's yours if you want it."

Dixon looked at him now, almost for the first time. "What's the matter with it?"

A swift anger came to Cass, but when he reflected on Dixon's question, he saw its reasonableness. Why, indeed, should the job go to him? Cass laughed suddenly. "You'll know in a week." He saw the unspoken question in Dixon's eyes, and he went on, "No, there's nothing wrong with it. It's easy money, so take it. You're just the man for it because you're a stranger. You don't know them, and you don't know the country, so you won't get mad at them. Remember that. Just don't get mad at them."

"Who?"

"This special agent and his surveyor," Cass said shortly. "About every two years the land office sends out another special agent. He's supposed to investigate reports of fraudulent entries for homesteads in this district. Hell, I can name twenty men who were crowded off their homesteads or were swindled out of them by the big cattle companies. I'm one myself. There must be a hundred, two hundred homesteads that they got illegally, one way or another. Every kid on the street knows the big outfits are stealing government land. But do these special agents ever turn up anything? No! The big outfits either kiss 'em to death or scare 'em to death." He reached in his pocket for money. "I'm tired of watching it, that's all. I know how it'll turn out."

He slapped a gold piece on the counter with unnecessary violence; even the thought of another special agent coming had already spoiled his day. He received his change, and shoved it in front of Dixon. "Buy yourself a new shirt and clean up. Meet the Vegas train at two. They're coming in this afternoon."

When Giff Dixon climbed the steps of the station platform, his long face freshly shaven and a clean shirt on his back, the scattering of men, mostly dressed in the half boots and range clothes of the cattle country, standing on the platform gave him a lingering look before turning their attention elsewhere. He was only a little taller than the ordinary man, but there was a kind of soft and bitter challenge in his long face that made a man wonder. It was a thin face, almost gaunt, and the full high cheekbones gave his dark eyes a deep watchfulness. A month indoors had bleach its weatherburn only a shade; the only place his skin

paled was at the edges of his thick black hair where
the barber had worked.

He chose a spot of sun by the paint-peeled station
wall, and because his knees still had a tendency to
bend too easily, he hunkered down against it on his
heels. The shimmering, endless plains to the east were
a pleasant thing to watch. Presently, he felt the fat
sack of new tobacco sagging in his shirt pocket. Although the pleasantly bitter taste of his last smoke was
still in his mouth, he slowly began to fashion a new
cigarette. Memory turned his thoughts again to this
morning's luck. The reasons for it he had not really
considered, and now he put his attention to them.

As he raised the cigarette to his lips, a shadow fell
across the planks in front of him, touching him. He
glanced up and saw a pleasant-faced man dressed in
a rumpled suit of black clothes and the black, narrow-
brimmed hat of a townsman standing before him. He
was gray-haired, on the small side, wore a mustache
clipped military fashion, and was somehow familiar.

"Aren't you the fellow they brought to me a month
or so ago?" the man asked in a friendly voice.

That would be the sheriff, Giff thought, and he nodded cautious acknowledgment.

"Doc said he'd turned you loose with a well freckled
belly."

Giff's smile held only a faint humor as he nodded
again.

Sheriff Edwards went on, "Normally, I'm not a curious man, but sometimes I'm supposed to be. These
Texas riders couldn't explain how you got shot. Can
you?"

Giff looked carefully down at his cigarette. "A hunting accident. I was shooting quail."

There was a moment of silence and Giff looked up
to see the corner of Edwards' mouth lifting in a faint
smile.

"With buckshot?"

"That's all I had."

"That's all the other fellow had, you mean. Who was
he?"

Giff again looked at his cigarette, and answered idly, "My horse. He wanted to get in a shot, but his hands were cold and he dropped the gun."

After a moment, he looked up again at the Sheriff. The smile was gone, and there was a faint flush on Edwards' face. There was something else there, too—not anger, only a kind of pity mixed with puzzlement before he turned and moved away.

That was a mistake, Giff thought narrowly. He realized too late of course that Edwards was asking only routine questions in a friendly way, much in the manner that Murray had quizzed him this morning. He remembered, also, that he had almost walked out on Murray because he'd resented his questioning too. In a bitter moment of self-knowledge, Dixon thought, *You damn fool, this is a new start. You don't have to be feisty now.*

The distant train, in sight now around the bend of the nearest foothill, whistled. Giff came to his feet and was still standing against the wall when the mixed train finally came to a halt at the dusty platform.

A half-dozen passengers descended from the lone passenger car and moved away. Then the brakeman, who had been standing beside the car on the platform, moved quickly up the steps. He backed down, holding a transit whose tripod was folded and lashed, and gently set it down. Then, piece by piece, duffel bags and luggage were handed down to him. Giff noticed then that the attention of every man on this platform was directed toward the passenger car steps, and he knew that all these men, for whatever reasons, were having their close look at the special agent.

When the agent finally descended, Sheriff Edwards went forward immediately, holding out his hand. Seeing him move, Giff remembered suddenly that the agent had written Edwards, and he thought bitterly, *Then my job will last two minutes longer.*

The agent was a stocky man in clean range clothes, and his smile was easy, almost professional as he shook Edwards' hand. His ruddy, loose face held a careless affability and the easy charm of the politician. It was the man behind him, however, who held Giff's interest. This man was older and wore a disreputable duck jacket, scuffed lace boots and a derby hat that had once been black but was now a mottled and sun-faded green. Ventilation holes had been punched just above its frayed hatband. His eyes were the palest gray under sandy eyebrows that bushed fiercely; his unsmiling face held the contained patience of a man who knew and liked his job and thought every minute away from it was a waste of time. Even his handshake was abrupt, Giff noticed, and then he thought resignedly, *Get it over with,* and walked over to the pile of luggage. He picked up the transit, and was reaching for a duffel bag when the older man saw him.

"Ho! You must be my chainman." He held out a rough hand. "Bill Fiske's the name."

Giff told him his and they shook hands. Sheriff Edwards had turned at the sound of their voices, and now he looked carefully at Giff. *Here it comes,* Giff thought, and he waited, watching Edwards with a still-faced defiance.

But Edwards only turned and said to the agent, "Welling, this is your guide, Giff Dixon."

Giff received the same friendly handshake and the identical affable smile. He noticed, though, that Welling's bloodshot eyes gave him a quick and shrewd appraisal.

Afterward, Giff loaded the luggage into the back of the hotel hack, and when the others were seated, he took a place in the back seat beside the gear.

There was talk, then, of the trip from Kansas City, all of it trivial, and then Giff heard Welling ask, "Where's Deyo? Out of town?"

"No, the train isn't very punctual, and the land office was busy this morning. He'll meet you at the hotel."

The Territory House, Corazon's only hotel, was a two-story adobe affair with a double veranda built at the town's main four corners. The hotel hack finished its quarter-mile journey from the station at the wide stepping block in front of the hotel steps. Giff was first down, and as he unloaded the luggage he saw the man come down the steps and approach them. He was a soft, well-barbered man of fifty, dressed in an expensive dark suit. The color in his sleekly jowled face came from good living, and not from the outdoors. There was a sort of bay rum elegance and arrogance about him that proclaimed his disdain for physical work.

Edwards said, "Here's your man, Welling. This is Ross Deyo. Vince Welling."

After acknowledging the introduction and introducing Fiske in turn, Welling said, "Where's a comfortable saloon, Sheriff? I'd like to buy you all a drink and talk with Deyo."

Fiske cut in dryly, "I can't take whiskey this early, Vince."

Welling laughed. "All right, you'll get a cigar. Only let's be comfortable."

Deyo mentioned the Plains Bar across from the livery, and they started across the street for it. Fiske paused long enough to say to Giff, "We wrote for rooms. Just lug the stuff up there." A faint humor wrinkled the skin at the corners of his eyes. "You drop that transit and you're dead." Without waiting for Giff's answer, he started across the dusty street after the others.

The room which the Territory House had reserved for them was a big corner one on the second floor facing Grant Street. Giff made two trips through the cool lobby and up the steps with the gear which he stored neatly in a corner of the room. Afterward, he moved to a window and looked out, musing. He decided he liked Fiske, who would be his real boss. Remembering Welling, his looks, his too easy manner, his eagerness for a saloon at this hour, Giff passed a narrow judgment on the man: he was a boozer and a lightweight. Recalling Cass's warning, *Just don't get mad at them,* he smiled faintly. *How can you get mad at nothing?*

He went out, and took to the stairs. There were horses to arrange for with Murray, and he wanted everything ready when he was asked about it.

The elderly clerk hailed him as he passed the desk

in the lobby. Extending an envelope to him, he said, "Give that to your boss, will you?"

"Which one?"

"Welling."

Giff nodded, pocketed the envelope and went out into the street, turning down it toward the livery. A mild traffic stirred on the street. A dozen horses were racked in front of the Plains Bar, and Giff guessed that the word was out that the special agent was on view there. A puncher driving three loose horses passed Giff; he halted to look at them, and afterward turned into the livery. Murray was not in the office, and Giff saw the hostler out in back hammering at the corral gate.

Giff tramped back to the corral and asked the ancient and dirty old man, "Where's Murray?"

The old man ceased hammering. "Farming, where he always is."

"Where's his place?" Giff asked curiously.

The old man smiled. "Hell, it ain't a farm, but he pretends it is. He's leased a half-block of town lots over east. He farms them half bushel crops just like they was three hundred acres. He can't keep away from growing things. It'll lose him his business, too, if he ain't careful."

Giff turned back and tramped up the runway. A pair of men were approaching him, the nearest, a big man in clean waist overalls, gray shirt and open vest. He was barely middle aged, Giff judged, although his full black mustaches were heavily threaded with gray. He was carrying his hat in his hand, and his thick black hair, parted deep on the side, held wide streaks of dead white. His handsome, ruddy face was weatherburned, but there were none of the telltale work lines, the brands of sun and wind, upon it. The almost benign expression on his face was somehow belied by the quiet arrogance in his dark eyes.

He was talking to his companion, a squat barrel of a man in soiled range clothes. He glanced at Giff, still talking as he drew abreast of him, and then he halted, ceased talking, and raised a large, well-fleshed hand to flag Giff down.

"Aren't you the fellow somebody told me was looking for a riding job?" His voice was oddly musical, and the expression in his eyes had altered to complete friendliness.

Giff nodded warily; instinct told him this was a persuasive man, and to be alert.

"Have you worked cattle much?"

"All my life."

"Then you're hired," the man said. "I'm short-handed now."

"You still are," Giff said. "I'm working."

"Who for?"

"The government. I'm chainman for the special agent's surveyor."

"And how long will that last?"

"I haven't asked."

The big man turned to his companion. "How long were the others here, Gus?"

"Oh, two weeks, maybe."

The big man turned back to Giff and said, "You're still hired, then. Just say I'm loaning you out to the government crew." He put out his hand. "I'm Sebree, Grady Sebree. This is Gus Traff, my foreman."

Giff shook hands with them both, then Sebree asked, "That all right with you?"

Giff didn't answer immediately, and then he said dryly, "This is a mighty changeable country, Mr. Sebree. For two days I've cruised the town looking for work. I've talked to men from most of the outfits and nobody is hiring, they told me. Now I'm offered two jobs in one day."

Sebree laughed easily. "Well, if you're a rancher, your men can get sick on you, and they can just plain quit on you. One quit on me last night, and another's sick." He paused. "Even if I hire another hand today, I'll need you in two weeks. Want the job?"

"If you want to wait," Giff said.

"Good. Oh, yes. You'd better pick up your saddle at Burtons." A kind of wry amusement crept into his blue eyes. "You'll need that, even working for the government. Tell Burton I sent you."

Giff nodded, and Sebree started to turn away, then checked himself. "Where are you surveying first?"

"Nobody's told me."

Sebree rubbed his cheek with the palm of his hand, looking off into space for a moment. "Tell you what. As soon as this agent fella' has made his plans, let me know, will you? I'd ask him myself, only I make a point of keeping myself and my men away from these agents. I don't want it thought I'm trying to influence them. As soon as their work is mapped out, I'd like to know what it is. I don't want any information that's private, and I don't want you to break a confidence, you understand."

There was no mockery in his tone, yet it was plain in his eyes, and when he finished speaking, a faint smile of irony lifted a corner of his mouth. Immediately, Giff understood the invitation, and he knew then why Sebree had hired him. The promise of a job had been held out to him, and he was getting his saddle back—this was in exchange for future information as to the plans of Welling, who probably intended to investigate him. Sebree had contrived to get this across to him by saying the exact opposite, and Giff had a brief and wary admiration for the man's cleverness. It was difficult to offer to buy a man without insulting him, yet Sebree had managed it. Giff had his choice of accepting or rejecting the offer without committing himself, which was what Sebree intended.

"All right," Giff said. Sebree gave him a parting smile and went on. Giff paused momentarily at the archway, then turned downstreet toward Burton's saddle shop. With a kind of cold amusement, he considered Sebree's proposition. Was he owing loyalty to a boozing politician who was probably incompetent, or to a man who had already done him a favor? *Wait and see,* he told himself cynically, *but first get the saddle.*

He passed a brick building on the corner which he noticed for the first time had Corazon District Land Office chiseled in the red sandstone lintel of the corner entrance, turned right, and went in to the adjoining building. Burton's dark and narrow shop, smelling of leather and oil and clean wood shavings, held a dozen saddles on sawhorses scattered in the front half of the shop.

An old man, unshaven and bent, was working on the wood of a saddletree at his bench. Leaning against the far end of it was a middle-aged puncher, moodily watching the old man work. Both turned as they heard Giff approach.

"Fellow name of Sebree told me to pick up my saddle, and he'd settle for it."

The old man pointed to a half-dozen saddles against the wall. "It's right where you dumped it."

Giff went over to his saddle, and then glanced up at the old man. "Who's this Sebree?"

The old man exchanged glances with the puncher before he smiled faintly and replied, "You're working for him, aren't you?"

"Not yet. In a few weeks I will be. But who is he?"

Again the old man glanced at the puncher, "Like to answer that, Les?"

The puncher regarded Giff morosely. "He pays standard wages. That's all you care about, isn't it?"

"Not all. Does he run a big or little outfit? Where's his place?"

A faint humor stirred in the puncher's sad eyes. "You point your horse northeast and ride two days and you'll still be on his land. Didn't you ever hear of the Torreon Cattle Company?"

Giff shook his head in negation and the puncher glanced wryly at the old man.

"Well, this whole damn town is just a Torreon loading pen. Everyone in it fits in Sebree's vest pocket with lots of room to spare."

Giff said dryly, "But not you?"

The puncher shook his head. "I tried it once but the climate didn't agree with me. I'm forty miles back in the mountains now and the air smells better."

Giff looked at the old man. "You feel that way about it too, Pop?"

The puncher said swiftly, "You were talking to me, weren't you?"

Giff understood then that where this maverick puncher could afford to speak the truth, old Burton could
not. He picked up his saddle, said, "Thanks, Pop,"
and went out. He was even surer, now, of Sebree's
reason for hiring him; when a man had a lot at stake,
bluntness was understandable.

He dumped his saddle in the livery office, then went
on upstreet to the hotel and climbed the stairs. At
Welling's door, he knocked and was bidden enter.
Fiske was already at work. He had cleared off the table
in the middle of the room, had a plat tacked down on
its surface and was bending over examining it. Welling
lay sprawled across the bed, his boots just off the
coverlet, and he was sleeping.

Fiske looked up, said "Hello," and went back to
his work. Giff took the envelope from his pocket and
laid it on the table. "You want me for anything?"

"No." Fiske straightened up, looking at the envelope.
"What's this?"

"The hotel clerk gave it to me to give to you."

Fiske opened the envelope, took out the letter and
read it. Finished, he gave Giff a searching glance, and
read it again. Then, still holding the letter in his hand,
he moved over to the bed. Putting a hand on Welling's
shoulder, he shook him roughly, and Welling sleepily
turned over. "What the hell, Bill?" Welling protested
sleepily.

"Go duck your head in the basin, and then read
this," Fiske said, holding out the letter.

Welling sat up, reached for the letter and yawned,
then gave it his half-fuddled regard. He read the letter
through, shook his head as if to clear it of whiskey
fumes, and read it through again. Then he looked over
at Giff, who was watching this with a rising, impersonal
curiosity. "Did you bring this?"

Giff told him about the clerk's handing it to him.

"Who's Perry Albers?" Welling asked.

"Careful, Vince," Fiske cut in.

Welling looked up at him, but Fiske was watching
Giff. "Why careful?"

"That letter was meant for you alone, and nobody else. Even I shouldn't have read it."

Welling regarded him for a stupefied moment, and then he laughed. "Bill, you're crazy—crazier than the fool who wrote this. This is a grudge letter. I get them everywhere I go."

"You don't believe it?"

"No."

"Then you're a damn fool," Fiske said quietly, finally.

Welling, far from being offended, scowled and looked again at the letter, then sighed, "All right, I'll go see him, then."

"If you do that, you'll likely get him shot," Fiske said dryly. "Why do you think he wrote you instead of coming to see you? He's being careful. In return, that's the least you can do."

Welling heaved himself to his feet and said petulantly, "First, I don't take the letter seriously enough. Then when I offer to, you stop me. Make some sense, Bill."

Fiske rammed his hands in his pockets and, head down, walked to the table, wheeled and came back. He raised his head sharply and regarded Giff. "No offense, Dixon. We don't know anything about you."

"That's right," Giff said indifferently. "I'll be down in the lobby if you want me." He moved toward the door, oddly relieved at a chance to escape.

"We want you right now," Fiske said flatly. He took the letter from Welling's hand, then went back to the table. From the letter, he copied something onto a piece of paper, picked up the letter and the paper and came over to Giff, who had halted at the door.

"You know what a final proof notice for a homestead entry is?" he asked.

"No."

Fiske explained to him that when a homesteader had lived on his homestead for six months of one year and had made the required improvements on it, he must publish notice for final proof in four consecutive issues of a newspaper, after which the publisher would sign an affidavit of publication for him to submit to the Register of the Land Office to complete his claim for title on the land. It was a newspaper form, Fiske said; surely he had seen the notices.

"I worked cattle. I didn't farm," Giff said. "I've seen them. I never paid any attention."

"Then pay attention now," Fiske said dryly, and he thrust the paper into Giff's hand. "Go down to the newspaper office. It's called"—here he referred to the letter—"the *San Dimas County Free Press*. Ask for their files. Hunt up the April seventeenth copy of last year. That paper I gave you has the names of five entrymen on it. See if their final proof notices are in that issue."

Wordlessly, Giff accepted the paper and put it in his pocket. Welling, behind Fiske, was looking sullen and still drowsy as he said, "Ask if their printer is named Perry Albers."

"Don't ask!" Fiske contradicted flatly. He turned to Welling. "What's the sense in all this if we let them know we're looking for Albers?"

"All right," Welling said sulkily. "It's damn foolishness anyway."

Giff asked patiently, "Am I supposed to do this on the quiet?"

"No. Land Office investigators are eternally at newspaper files. Everybody knows it. Just don't tell them what issue you want."

Giff went out, then, and descended to the lobby. He was amused and curious about what had just happened, but not overly. It was obvious that Perry Albers, the *Free Press* printer, had written them information Fiske thought valuable and Welling did not.

In his first chore on the new job, Giff reflected, it had been Fiske who made the decision, and Welling, fuddled with liquor, who fell into line with it. Oddly, Giff did not hold Fiske's suspicion of him against the older man; remembering Sebree's offer, he thought, *Fiske's right. Why tell me anything?* He was used to hard judgments, and took no affront.

The newspaper office was a narrow building wedged

between two larger ones, and was in the block past the land office on the opposite side of the street. Its big window was painted white to half its height, on which in black, big letters was printed *San Dimas County Free Press*.

Stepping in from the sun-drenched street, Giff halted and closed the door, his eyes slowly adjusting themselves to the gloom of the long room. Presently, he made out a big flat-topped desk against the window. A couple of chairs, a tall clothes commode and a rusty safe made up the furniture. The room was in monumental disorder, the desk littered with papers, the floor cluttered with boxes and cartons, piled almost to the ceiling with bound files and yellowing newspapers.

The only sound came from the print shop in the rear where an overhead lamp was burning, and it was strange sound, the rapid chinking of metal against metal. Giff walked up to a tall cabinet whose back was to the street, and rounding it, came to an abrupt halt. A girl, wearing an ink-stained and oversized apron, was seated on a tall stool setting type; her hands moved with sure swiftness as she selected the type from the case and slapped it into the stick in the left hand.

Giff watched her a moment in mild wonderment, and then started as she addressed him in total unfriendliness without interrupting her work or even looking at him. "What do you want?"

His surprise held him mute a moment; the girl, getting no answer, ceased work and looked up at him, her face harried and without patience. When she saw him, her expression altered to one of mocking apology without any embarrassment at all. She was a small girl, almost frail-seeming, and her dark and curly hair was pinned in an unruly mass atop her head. Her green eyes, wide-spaced and direct, seemed large because of her small nose, and now her full lips relaxed in a crooked smile.

"I thought you were Earl," she said, and leaned both hands on the type case. "Anyway, what is it you want?"

"I'd like a look at your back numbers," Giff said cautiously.

The girl sighed wearily. "You picked a time, didn't you?"

"Did I?"

"The worst," the girl said tartly. "The boss is shooting billiards over in the saloon. He's stepping over the printer, who's probably lying drunk on the floor. I've got a paper to get out, and who gives a damn about it besides me?"

Giff frowned a little in distaste, and the girl looked sharply at him. "Haven't you ever heard a girl swear?"

"None like you."

"You don't see any of them doing my job either, do you?" she asked with instant truculence. When Giff didn't answer, she shifted her attention to the type case and stared at it for a moment. Then she said, "Did you see that broken down coat closet in the office? Well, pull a chair up to it, and *don't* put a foot through the chair seat when you stand on it. The bound files are on top of the closet. Take them down and *don't* pull down all that trash on top." She grinned faintly, then, and added, "And keep out of my way or I'll stomp on you."

"Yes, ma'am," Giff said dryly.

His jibe was entirely lost on the girl; she was setting type again. Giff turned back into the office, a faint resentment at her stirring in him. *She'll make some man a fine husband,* he thought. Nevertheless, he followed her instructions, being careful not to put his foot through the worn cane bottom of the chair.

Lugging the files over to the desk, he cleared a space among the papers, and while the soft chunk-chunking noise of the girl's typesetting went on, he looked through the files. First, he identified the form of a final proof notice. Then he looked for last year's April seventeenth issue of the paper, and found it missing. Curious now, he leafed back and found other issues missing, even into the year before and the year before that. His search had come to full stop, and he speculated a moment on the reason for their absence. He shrugged then, and put the files back where they belonged. He'd done his job, and the results meant nothing to him.

Curiosity, however, drew him back to the girl. He stood patiently by the type stand while she finished a stick, and then she looked up at him inquiringly.

"Don't you keep a copy of all the issues of your paper?" he asked.

"In summer, we do. Then when winter comes, we have to have something to start fires." When Giff didn't smile, she said, "You're a gay lad, aren't you? That was a joke, but don't smile for me."

Giff shifted uncomfortably, watching her. She sighed and said, "What was it? Maybe I can remember it."

Recalling Fiske's words, Giff said idly, "Oh, land office stuff. We have to look up a lot of it."

The girl set down the stick of type gently, carefully, a sudden interest coming into her eyes. "Don't tell me you're that new boozehead agent by the name of Welling?"

"The name is Dixon," Giff said coldly. "I'm working for Welling."

"Well, happy headaches," she murmured softly. "Here we go again." She looked carefully at him. "Haven't I seen you around? Yesterday, say? With fur on your face?"

Giff nodded stiffly. "I've been here a month, staying at Doc Miller's."

"Oh, the clay pigeon," she said. "Well, well, at least you've had some practice."

"What does that mean?"

"Getting shot at," the girl said unemotionally.

Before he could reply, he heard the door shut behind him. At the sound of it, the girl raised her head and called, "Earl!" There was a grunt from the office, followed by the slamming of a drawer, then footsteps. At the other side of the type stand, a man appeared and halted. He was a thin, tall, mournful-looking man dressed in an unpressed black suit; his hat, pushed far back on his head, revealed a bald, bony skull. His face was sharp and almost cadaverous. Carefully, he tucked a handful of cigars into the breast pocket of his coat, regarding the girl.

"Where's Perry?" she demanded.

"Why—here, isn't he?" Earl answered idly.

"Why do you think I'm setting type if he is?" the girl demanded angrily. "Where's your billard game this afternoon?"

"Reno's."

"Then he's likely flat on his face at Henty's!" she said angrily. She raised the stick of type and shook it at him. "I'll set this up, since he's probably so drunk he can't. But if you think I'm going to run that press to-morrow, you're crazy!"

Earl raised both thin hands in protest. "All right, all right, I'll get a boy in."

"Get Perry in! He's your printer! You pay him! Leave your billiard game long enough to lug him out of that saloon and sober him up!"

"Oh, I haven't time," Earl said idly. He looked without interest at Giff, then turned and started out.

"I hope you choke on chalk dust!" the girl called angrily. "I hope you get a sliver up to your elbow. I hope—" but the slamming of the door then cut her off. She turned back to the type stand then, and saw Giff. "Are you still here?" she demanded angrily.

Giff watched her a moment, then said, "Tell me something."

"No! All right, what?"

"Can you whisper?"

Amazingly, then, the girl broke into laughter. She threw her head back and laughed with a kind of wild and antic joy that brought an infectious grin to Giff's still face.

When her laughter had subsided, she said, "I had that coming, didn't I? Yes, I can whisper, but to hear me you'll have to pick a day that's not before press day and when the printer isn't drunk and the publisher isn't shooting billiards." She regarded him with friendliness, "Do me a favor, Mr. Dixon. Go over to Henty's and if our printer is standing up, turn him this way and give him a shove, will you?"

"How do I know him?"

"Black hands," she said flatly. Giff touched his hat and went out. Pausing a moment on the boardwalk to roll a cigarette, he found himself wondering at memory of this girl. His thoughts sobered, however, when he remembered her last words before Earl's entrance. Was it a prediction, or just the flip observation of a harried girl? At any rate, he had part of the information Fiske wanted: the printer's first name was Perry, which would be Albers, and learning it had been done without rousing suspicion.

He identified Henty's saloon on the corner across from the land office, and stepping out into the street, he cut through the late afternoon traffic of wagons and riders and fell in behind two punchers preceding him into the saloon.

It was a big and pleasant place, with the bar directly ahead of the door. In the back were two billiard tables, and the rest of the room was reserved for a faro layout and half a dozen big poker tables. Three separate card games were in progress, and a handful of drinkers stood at the bar.

Giff went to the bar and had his drink of whiskey, the first in more than a month. He could not afford it, but he also could not afford not to, for he did not want it to appear as if he were hunting anyone. In fact, he had no intention of doing the girl the favor she had requested; he simply wanted to see Albers and be able to describe him to Fiske. He was amused at his own sudden interest in this preposterous game of Fiske's.

Finished with his drink, he drifted over to a poker table and, along with another puncher, watched the game a moment. His glance roved the room. Presently, he observed a man at a table in the front corner; he was half stretched out on the table, sleeping on his arms, but across the room Giff could not make out his features.

He moved on, then, to another game at a table next to the corner one, approaching it so that when he turned away he would pass the corner table. Halting, he idly noted the men playing, and then his glance settled on Sebree's foreman across the table. Traff had seen him, and Giff nodded his greeting and had it returned.

He watched Traff a moment, wondering about him. He had a broad face, with wide flaring nostrils and small eyes; his neck was nonexistent, so that his massive shoulders seemed to flow away from his ears, and yet seated, he was inches shorter than the men he was playing with. His very grossness suggested power and drive, and his every move held authority. This was the man who might be his boss.

Raising his glance now, Traff surprised Giff watching him. He nodded to the empty chair next to him and asked, "Like to sit in?"

Giff shook his head and smiled faintly. "I've got my saddle back. I'd like to keep it."

Traff grinned. Giff watched a hand played out, then idly turned away. With seeming naturalness, he looked at the figure sprawled on the next table. There were the ink-stained hands, all right, cradling the man's head. His face, mouth open, was turned to the room and Giff had his casual look at him on the way out.

Dusk lay over the town when he stepped into the street and the earliest lamps were being lighted. Giff, on his way to the hotel, paused long enough to see if Murray was in, found he wasn't, and walked on. The lobby lamps of the Territory House were already lighted, and the dining room adjoining was open.

Giff had climbed two of the steps to the second story when he stopped abruptly, thought of something, turned and came back to the desk. The elderly clerk had seen him, and came out of his chair as Giff approached the counter.

"That letter you gave me this afternoon. Who gave it to you?" Giff asked.

"Some kid."

And now he asked the question that had brought him here. "Do you know a girl working in the *Free Press* office?"

"Mary Kincheon, sure."

Giff turned toward the stairs, turning over the name

in his mind, liking the sound of it and wondering why he did. At his knock, Fiske's abrupt voice told him to come in. Fiske had pulled a chair over to a window on the side street; he was sitting in it, feet up on the sill, smoking a huge calabash pipe. Giff walked around the table, noting Welling's absence, swung a straight chair away from the wall, straddled it, folded his arms on the back and sat down.

"Albers works there, right enough," he reported. "Right now, he's sleeping off a jag on a corner table of Henty's saloon. The April seventeenth copy was missing, so I couldn't check these names." He extended the slip of paper to Fiske, who took it without comment. When Fiske held his silence, Giff rose. "That's all?"

"Going to sleep in the hayloft again tonight?" Fiske asked mildly.

Giff peered at him in the dusk, and he knew Fiske was watching his face. "Hayloft?"

"While you were checking on Albers, I was checking on you," Fiske said dryly. "Nobody knows anything about you. Murray seems to think you're all right."

When Giff didn't answer, Fiske said grimly, "I hope you are." He rose. "Seen Welling?"

"No."

"He's taking the weight off the back bar of the saloon across the street. Have you already gathered that's his real career?"

"Yes."

Fiske turned away from the chair and made a slow circle of the room, his head hung thoughtfully. When the circle touched Giff, he halted. "I've got no authority and you're only a harum-scarum camp swamper as far as I can find out. Something's happening here, though, something big—and we two are the only ones who can do anything about it. Feel like trying?"

"What is it?" Giff asked cautiously.

"That's none of your business. It's none of mine either, but I'm making it mine. Want to take it that way—blindfolded?"

Many things ribboned through Giff's mind then— Sebree and the price he might be eager to pay for information, Mary Kincheon's warning, Fiske's description of Welling. He felt no loyalty to this barb-tongued surveyor who admitted he was snooping in business that didn't concern him. His only loyalty was to Murray, who didn't give a damn about either the agent or his surveyor. But a kind of wary curiosity nagged at him. Beyond that, he sensed the almost desperate tone in Fiske's words. *What's there to lose?* he thought then. Too, the thought that Fiske didn't trust him, and rightly, was upon repetition beginning to smart.

He said tonelessly, "What do I do?"

"Get Albers up here without anyone knowing it."

Giff thought about that a moment, cautiously turning it over in his mind. That shouldn't be hard, once Albers sobered up. "All right," he said.

Fiske talked then, pointing out a way to accomplish it. Once the card players came into Henty's after supper and the tables filled, Albers would be moved. The thing to do was wait for his exit, follow him, and bring him up the backstairs fire escape. Fiske, meanwhile, would undertake to get Welling from the saloon.

"Two drunks," Giff said coldly. "What sense will they make?"

"You'll never know," Fiske countered tartly. "Just get him here."

They left the lobby together and parted in front of the stepping block in the new dark. Giff moved downstreet to the corner, crossed it, and entered Henty's saloon. The evening crowd was gathering. Without stepping up to the bar, Giff saw Albers still asleep at the corner table. Traff was still playing in his game too.

Giff went out, crossed the street, and took up his vigil in the dark recess of the land office doorway. He did not have long to wait, for within a matter of minutes he saw one of the white-aproned bartenders push open the batwings. He had a man by the arm, and he gently stood him up, balanced him, and then vanished into the saloon. In the light coming over the swingdoors, Giff recognized Albers.

The printer lurched out to the edge of the plankwalk, caught himself, and with a careful steadiness, stepped into the road and cut across it and down the side street west. Giff waited a moment, keeping him in sight, then stepped out and cut down the side street too, keeping to the walk. When Albers turned up the alley that ran behind the *Free Press,* Giff hurried across the street and plunged in after him.

Ahead, he could hear Albers stumbling among the cinders, and could see his vague shape. He called softly, "Albers," and started to run toward him. Albers moaned softly, and he too began to run, and then he fell heavily. When he rose, Giff was beside him, and Albers struck out blindly, yelling, "No! No! I didn't, I tell you!"

Roughly, Giff pinned the man's arms, and then said through his teeth, "Stop it, you damn fool! I'm from the Land Office!"

Albers stopped struggling, and Giff let him go. "Come along," Giff said. "Welling sent me for you."

At that moment, the sound of running feet came to him, and he looked back down the alley. A couple of men rounded into it, running full tilt. Albers heard them, too, and he swore bitterly, drunkenly, and began to run again. Giff ran alongside him, wondering what to do, how to hide him.

Then the shot boomed savagely in the enclosed alley. It was the second one, though, that hit Albers. Giff could tell by the sound of gagging wind driven from him that the bullet had hit him in the back. He fell heavily, loosely. For only a moment, Giff paused, then ran again, the end of the alley in sight.

He pounded around the corner of the building, his foot lifted to achieve the boardwalk, when the thing hit him. It was as if he had run full tilt into an eight by eight timber; it caught him in the belly, and he had time only to see the blurred figure of a man beside him. Then he was down, gagging and retching, while the kicks and blows were rained on his head and body. Finally, mercifully, a kick in his temple seemed to explode the night into pinwheeling fire, and he lost himself in blackness.

2

ALTHOUGH WELLING was still sleeping, Bill Fiske made no effort to be quiet as he dressed and shaved the next morning. There were things more important than Welling's sleep, and one of them was Giff Dixon, Fiske thought. He let himself out of the room and tramped down the corridor, heading for the room to which Dixon, beaten up and bloody, had been brought last night.

His soft knock on the door brought no response, and gently he palmed the knob and opened the door. Dixon was gone, and for a moment Fiske stood in the doorway, a gloom settling upon him. *He likely lit out, and I can't blame him,* he thought.

Turning back down the hall, his feeling of guilt deepened. Without even knowing what he was in for, Dixon had volunteered to help last night; and a brutal beating had been his reward. That, of course, finished Dixon; with him gone Fiske could see certain and unpleasant failure on this job, since the only thing reliable about Welling was his thirst.

Tramping down the steps, he nodded good morning to the day clerk at the desk and then turned into the dining room on the right. A scattering of guests and townsmen were at breakfast—and among them, Fiske saw, was Dixon. Even across the room, he could see the purple bruise on Dixon's right cheekbone extending clear to the temple. As he approached, Fiske recognized the man sitting at Giff's table. It was Sheriff Edwards who, of course, would be at Giff again with his questions. Fiske had no notion if the young man would tell the truth to the sheriff. It didn't matter much one way or the other, for the harm was already done.

He halted beside Giff, who looked up at him without much friendliness. "Who helped you out of bed?" Fiske asked gruffly.

"Cass Murray."

Uninvited, Fiske pulled out a chair, saying, "Morning, Sheriff. Anything new on Albers' killing?"

"Nothing new, and nothing old," Edwards answered dispiritedly. "Just plain nothing." He glanced at Dixon now and rose. "The hearing will be in an hour or so at my store. Doesn't make much sense, since you're about the only witness, but we ought to go through with it."

Dixon nodded, and Edwards moved away. The waitress was waiting, and Fiske gave his order; then put his elbows on the table and glanced at Dixon, who was finished with his breakfast and was now rolling a smoke, his long face morose with suppressed anger. "What'd you tell him?"

"That I was helping a drunk when we got jumped."

"Think he believed it?"

"He may, but I don't," Dixon's glance, almost baleful, settled on Fiske. "Your drunken friend was shooting his mouth off in the Plains Bar saloon yesterday evening. He told the whole saloon he was ready to break open a big land swindle—just as soon as we got in contact with a man."

Fiske asked unbelievingly, "Who heard him say it?"

"Cass Murray. So did everybody else."

Fiske felt a hot and overwhelming wrath that almost smothered him, and he leaned back in his chair. He was aware of too many things at once—that he could now point to Albers' killer and that Welling's loose talk had brought about the killing. He was also aware that Dixon was still in the dark as to the reasons for his beating; and the memory of his suspicion of Dixon yesterday brought a wrenching shame to him.

The waitress brought his breakfast then, but he regarded it without hunger, ate a little of it and finally pushed it aside. There was a feeling in him that was close to futility; their errand here was useless, even foolish; he was useless, foolish, too.

Glancing up, he surprised Dixon watching him with a sullen, almost bitter, patience. Fiske asked, "How do you feel?"

"I'd feel a lot better if I understood this."

Fiske grimaced. "You wouldn't, and I'll prove it." He leaned both hands on the table and said, "You already know it was Albers who sent that note to Welling."

Giff nodded.

"Did you ever hear of a rancher here by the name of Sebree, Grady Sebree? He's manager and biggest stockholder in the Torreon Cattle Company."

Giff said flatly, "Yes."

Fiske looked surprised. "What do you know about him?"

"Well, in the space of five minutes yesterday I met one man scared to death of him and another who'd run from him. Why?"

"Well, Albers' letter accused Sebree along with Earl Kearie, the *Free Press* publisher, and Ross Deyo of being in on a tremendous land swindle. You remember Deyo's the man we were introduced to outside yesterday, the register for the local land office?"

Dixon was watching him with surly attention.

"The swindle works this way: Sebree has his riders file homestead entries on waterholes and springs that his company wants. Deyo obligingly predates the entries for the land office records, and Sebree's cowboys swear that his phony entrymen have lived on the land and improved it. But before a title can be given for any homestead, the land office and the public have got to see proof of publication—that is, a legal form printed in a newspaper stating that so-and-so has filled all homestead requirements for a certain piece of land. That's where Kearie comes in."

Dixon was watching him, listening closely.

"Kearie has his printer run off an ordinary issue of the *Free Press*. But the type is left set up afterwards. Then Kearie has his printer—Albers in this case—lift out some advertisements and insert in their place the fraudulent final proof notices of Sebree's riders. He runs off two copies only, then destroys the type."

Giff scowled. "Who are they for?"

"One for Sebree, and one for Deyo. Deyo has to file proof notices in Washington. Kearie takes one of these phony issues over to a crooked J.P. named Arnold. Kearie fills out an affidavit of publication swearing that these notices appeared in four consecutive issues of his paper. Arnold notarizes it. Then Kearie takes the affidavit and the phony paper to Deyo. Since everything appears in proper order to Deyo—after all, he sees a copy of the paper with his own eyes—Deyo passes them on to the Land Office in Washington. Pretty soon, Sebree's riders get a certificate of title to the homesteads. If anybody is interested enough to kick when they find Sebree suddenly owns that land, the land office records are trotted out." Fiske shrugged. "There's the certificate of title which Washington wouldn't have granted unless everything was legal, Deyo says. Certainly final proof notices were published. Just hunt up a copy of the *Free Press* and see for yourself."

"Where does a man get a copy of a month-old newspaper?" Giff asked.

"At the newspaper office," Fiske said dryly. "And he gets the same story you got yesterday. 'No, we haven't got a copy of that issue. It's gone.' "

Dixon was silent a long moment, and then he asked skeptically, "Could it be done?"

"I never heard of it, but it could," Fiske said grimly. "Anyway, Albers wrote Welling that's the way it worked."

"And Albers is dead."

Fiske looked at him a long moment, then nodded. "What more proof do you need that it worked?"

"So Sebree's the man who killed him, the man who had me beat up?"

"Sebree, Deyo or Kearie."

It's Sebree, all right, Giff thought thinly. It all meshed perfectly, from Sebree's hiring him in hopes he could get inside information down to the beating he received last night for butting into something that wasn't his business.

Giff's voice had a rough edge to it as he asked, "If you knew all this already from what Albers wrote, why did you send me to get him?"

"No good reason," Fiske said wearily. "In his letter, Albers said he once had two copies of the April seventeenth *Free Press* for last year—one a true run copy, the other a fixed-up phony—and that they'd been stolen from him."

"Who stole them?" Giff asked skeptically.

"That's what I wanted to ask him—if he had any idea who could have them. I'm sorry I sent you."

Some of Giff's truculence fell away at Fiske's disarming honesty. He wanted to clear up the rest of it now, and he asked, "What if I'd found the April seventeeth issue in the *Free Press* files?"

"That would have proved Albers' charge."

"I don't see how."

Fiske spread his hands. "Because the phony final proof notices of those five men are in the land office records in Washington. We could get them. If we found a true run copy of the April seventeenth *Free Press* and found those proof notices weren't in it, we'd prove fraud. Sebree, Deyo and Kearie would go to jail."

Giff understood it now. He asked, "What's so hard about finding a copy? There must be one somewhere outside of the newspaper files."

"Who saves fifteen-month-old newspapers?"

"Advertise and ask."

"In Kearie's own newspaper?" Fiske asked coldly. "No, nobody keeps old newspapers except a newspaper itself. Since we can't ask everyone to look in their woodsheds, it's pretty hopeless, isn't it?"

Giff supposed that was true and was silent, but anger was still in him. In spite of Fiske's candor, he had the feeling that he had been used. He had been offered a simple work hand's job, and had accepted it in order to eat. In the space of one short day, he had become involved in an intrigue he had no taste for, and had got a beating for his pains. *Not a beating, a kicking,* he

thought bitterly. The thing to do now was pull out, quit.
He had his saddle, and he'd paid for it by taking his
beating. He owed none of these people any loyalty, and
Cass, once he understood, would not blame him for
quitting. No, he'd borrow a horse from Cass and ride
out today.

Fiske drank his coffee and then reached in his
pocket for his pipe. Stuffing it with shaggy tobacco he
seemed to carry loose in his jacket pocket, he regarded
Giff frowningly. "I suppose you're through working
for the government."

Giff nodded. "You can get another packer easy."

Fiske sighed. "Don't blame you." He lighted his
pipe, and then said, "You'll have to go to the hearing."

"All right."

"I'll see you afterward and pay you."

Giff rose. "What do I say at the hearing?"

"Just what you've told Edwards."

Giff accepted that and tramped out. Once on the
street, he turned toward the livery, wondering where
Edwards' store was. Already there was a feeling of
relief upon him at his decision to leave. He'd left a job
working for a drunken fool and near helpless old man
at a job whose deadly danger he was only beginning to
realize. He had worked long enough in the bitter anony-
mity of the trail drives to know that his life was
valuable only to him. Here in this strange town, he was
a saddle tramp with only a name to distinguish him
from other broke drifters. Nobody would question his
death, or if they did, the questioning would cease at
Sebree's command.

Passing Henty's saloon, he had not seen a store
marked Edwards. He halted, about to ask directions
from a man approaching when his glance fell on the
Free Press office.

Remembering his conversation with Fiske, a kind of
perversity settled upon him as he regarded the sign.
What was it Fiske had said when he suggested ad-
vertising for the missing copy of the *Free Press? In
Kearie's own newspaper?* Giff was remembering Mary
Kincheon's remarks about Kearie's total indifference to

his publication. It just might work, he thought, and stepped off into the street, heading for the *Free Press* office.

Mary Kincheon, apronless and neat, was seated at the front desk. She wore a dark blue serviceable dress, and was bent over the desk writing. Paper cuffs protected her sleeves, and Giff could hear them scratching as she wrote.

Looking up, presently, she smiled and leaned back in her chair, regarding him with a swift mockery. "The clay pigeon," she exclaimed. "You're off to a good start, so I hear. Who pasted all that pretty color on your face?"

Giff felt a faint irritation at her words, but he dredged up a grin. He noted as he walked over to the desk that the press in the rear was silent, and he thought *Maybe it'll work*.

"There was sand on my pillow."

She regarded him levelly, her face altering into soberness. "They're just playing patty-cake now. Wait until they get serious."

"Who is 'they'?"

She shrugged. "Why, whoever gave you that. Do *you* know?"

"No. They won't do it again, either." He asked, then, before she could comment, "Is the paper printed?"

"Hah!"

Giff waited, then asked, "What does that mean?"

"It means is isn't. It means it won't be until Kearie remembers he owns a newspaper."

"Can I get something in it?"

The girl frowned. "What's so importatnt around here it can't wait a week? Land office business?"

At Giff's nod, she rose and started back to the print shop. Falling in behind her, Giff noticed how straight she carried herself, and he wondered suddenly *Is she in with Kearie?* He would know in a minute, he thought, as she paused by the type case, picked up a composing stick, and rested both hands on the stand. "What is it, now? It better be short."

"Head it 'Fifty Dollars Reward,' " Giff directed.

Her hands moved so swiftly it was only seconds before she looked up at him, ready, and he went on, "Will be paid for a complete April seventeenth, 1882, issue of the *San Dimas County Free Press* by V. Welling, Territory House, Corazon."

For a long moment her hands were motionless, and Giff could not tell if she were memorizing, or making up her mind to refuse the advertisement. When she looked up at him, her face was composed. "What's so special about the April seventeenth issue of last year?"

"They didn't tell me," Giff said idly.

She hesitated another long moment, then her hands went into swift action. Giff felt a faint elation. He was past the worst part, the accepting of the advertisement. With any luck, the paper would be printed and distributed before Kearie ever saw the item, and then it would be too late to do anything about it.

He waited until Mary Kincheon had finished, then watched her move over to the composing stone, unlock the forms, pull a filler out, insert the advertisement and lock the forms. When she was finished, he said, "Welling will stop by and pay you."

Mary nodded and observed acidly: "From what I hear, you'll have to count it out for him and tie it in a handkerchief. Why do you work for him?"

"Food."

"I understand." She gave him a brief and friendly smile before he turned and tramped out.

Of the first passerby he inquired for Edwards' and was told it was a hardware store across the street from the hotel. Retracing his steps, he felt an odd sense of satisfaction. He would be long gone out of town when the advertisement appeared this afternoon. If it did Fiske any good, he was welcome to it. If it did Sebree harm that was fine, too. In a way, it would compensate for the beating.

Entering Edwards', he was told by a clerk that the hearing was to be held in a back room. He went to the back of the store and behind the counter to the left he stepped through an open door into a large room containing folding chairs facing a table at which a

slack-faced elderly man sat. He was in conversation
with Sheriff Edwards, who had a leg up on the table.

A dozen or so men besides Welling and Fiske were
scattered around the room in several groups; Gus Traff
was talking to a pair of men in the far corner, and
he did not look at Giff as he entered.

Giff spied Cass Murray sitting alone on a chair toward the front of the room, his arms folded, a generous
chew of tobacco pouching his cheek. There was something lonely and independent and be-dammed-to-you
about the man that Giff did not wholly understand,
but he liked him. When he slipped into the chair beside
Cass, ignoring both Welling and Fiske, Cass turned
and winked solemnly at him.

"You've got something better to do than this," Giff
suggested.

Cass grimaced. "As a taxpayer I got a right to be
entertained. It's always the same; nobody'll know nothing." He looked levelly at Giff. "You know anything?"

The answer to that question was what had brought
Cass to his room early this morning, Giff knew. It
was a question he had ducked, mostly because he had
not known if Fiske wanted him to talk. Now he ducked
it again, but for another reason. "Wait and see," he said.

Before Cass could probe further, Giff asked, "Who's
at the desk?"

"Arnold, the J.P."

Edwards called out six names now of men who were
in the crowd of loafers, among them Gus Traff, and
these men filed up to the six chairs set along the wall.
They were the jury for the murder hearing.

Only now did Gus Traff look at Giff. It was a long,
down-bearing look holding a kind of careless triumph
that Giff readily understood. He remembered that Gus
Traff had been watching Albers all through the afternoon; it was doubtless Traff who shot Albers—or who
waited at the alley mouth to administer Giff's kicking.
Giff felt a slow wrath uncoil inside him as he held
Traff's glance, and then Sebree's foreman looked away.

The proceedings that followed were informal to the
point of carelessness. Arnold stated the purpose of the

investigation was to determine the cause of Perry Albers' death. He called him "Albert" and pronounced his first name "Peery" and Sheriff Edwards, bored, did not correct him.

As Arnold droned on, an idea slowly grew within Giff. It was, he knew, a reckless one, but he knew he was going to carry it out.

The first witness was Henty's bartender, who had not bothered to remove his apron. His testimony was brief. Around eight-thirty he had removed Albers from the premises because he was using up a poker table that was wanted for a game. The removal had been gentle, he insisted.

Giff was called then and took the chair in front of the table facing Arnold. This was the man, he remembered, who notarized Kearie's perjured affidavits of publication according to Fiske. He was a long-jawed, long-faced, old man, dirty and slack-eyed, and his air of petty authority did not become him.

Once Giff had given his name, his occupation as land office packer, his age as thirty, he was asked to tell what had happened last night. Talking easily he told about stopping on Henty's corner to watch Albers' progress from the saloon. The man was so drunk, he said, that he needed help, and he gave it to him. Halfway down the alley they heard men running toward them. No, he didn't recognize any of them, Albers did, though, and began to run.

"Albert did?" Arnold cut in. "How do you know that?"

Giff made the plunge. "From what he said."

"And what was that?"

"He said, 'Help me. Grady's after me,' " Giff lied calmly.

There was a long moment of utter silence during which Giff looked levelly at Arnold. He saw Arnold's brief frightened glance at Gus Traff, and then the J.P. swiveled his glance back to him. It was Edwards, however, who found his voice first.

"Do you know any Grady here, Dixon? Do you know who he was talking about?"

"No."

"Go on," Arnold said hurriedly. "Then what happened?"

"We ran, and then there were two shots. Albers fell. I didn't have a gun and there was no way I could help him, so I ran for the head of the alley. They were waiting for me there as I turned into the street."

"What happened?"

"I got beat up and kicked," Giff said thinly.

Arnold's next question was asked offhandedly, reluctantly, "Have you any idea who did it?"

"Only the name of the man who ordered it done," Giff said calmly.

"How do you know that?" Arnold pounced on him.

"From what I heard them say."

Arnold looked pleadingly at Edwards and then away. He didn't want to ask the next question, but he had to. "What did they say?"

"One said, 'That him?' and the other said, 'He's the one Gus said.' That's all I remember because someone kicked me in the head then."

Again there was a long and ominous silence, and then Sheriff Edwards said, "Judge, I'd suggest we put this witness under oath. We've been too informal by the looks of things."

Arnold looked at him blankly, and then Edwards' intent seemed to dawn on him. He looked wrathfully at Giff, opened a drawer in his desk, took a Bible from it and then said sternly, "Stand up!"

Giff did, and was sworn in, then sat down. Arnold looked questioningly at Edwards, who was watching Giff. Edwards said, "Go back to what Albers said in the alley. What did he?"

Giff knew he'd been caught and he didn't care much, for he had accomplished what he had set out to do. Just what that was he didn't frame in words, but he had intended it as a parting shot at Sebree and Traff. His listeners could read into it anything they wished, but the facts which he was retracting were nevertheless true, and he hoped they knew it.

He said indifferently, "Albers said, 'No. No, I didn't!' "

"Know what he meant?" Edwards prodded gently. "No."

"Now go back to the attack on you. Did you hear any talk while you were being beat up?"

"None."

"Your witness, Judge," Edwards said dryly.

There was a crash of talk in the room then, and Arnold pounded the table for silence. The talk subsided, and Judge Arnold turned his attention to Giff; he had his mouth open to speak when someone in the rear of the room said loudly, "If it please your honor."

The voice was Welling's, Giff knew without turning to look. Arnold's gaze lifted, and Giff saw the bitter dislike in it as Arnold asked sourly, "What is it?"

"On behalf of the Land Office I would like to disclaim any responsibility for Dixon's testimony. He was instructed to cooperate with the county officials in every way."

Arnold said coldly, "Is that all?"

"Yes, your honor." Welling's tone was fawning, respectful, and a soft murmur of amused laughter came from the back of the room. Even Arnold smiled.

Then his face altered to sternness again, and he returned his glance to Giff, "I don't suppose there's anything I can do to you since you told the truth under oath. But I warn you, you're headed for trouble. Murder is a serious business."

"Beginning when?" Giff asked disinterestedly.

"Step down!" Arnold ordered angrily.

"Just a minute," a voice put in. It was Gus Traff's and he was looking at Arnold. "Is a juryman allowed to question a witness?"

"Of course," Arnold said. "We're only trying to get at the truth, no matter how."

Traff looked at Giff and said slowly, "You might tell the real reason you're so anxious to involve Mr. Sebree and me in trouble—any kind of trouble."

He didn't wait for Giff to answer, but addressed

Arnold. "He walked into Burton's saddle shop yesterday, claimed he was working for Torreon, and took his saddle that he'd sold Burton. He told Burton Sebree would pay him for it." Now he looked levelly at Giff and said, "Mr. Sebree never saw him before. He never promised him a job, and never told him to pick up his saddle from Burton. Know what I think?"

He was looking at Arnold now, and Arnold said, "What?"

"I think he used a saddle tramp's gall to steal back his saddle. I think he's trying to blacken Mr. Sebree's character now, beforehand, so that when Mr. Sebree turns the saddle stealing over to the sheriff's office, he can point to his own lying evidence here as proof that Mr. Sebree is a liar and that his word is not to be trusted."

Arnold slowly turned his head to look at Giff. "What have you got to say to that?"

"Nothing you'd listen to," Giff said.

Arnold glared at him a moment, then said, "Step down."

Giff rose, his glance falling briefly on Gus Traff. Traff's eyes met his, and they held a look of sleepy malice, of unworried patience and of triumph. Instead of taking his seat again beside Cass, Giff started on through the room toward the doorway into the store.

"Oh, Dixon."

It was the sheriff's voice, and Giff halted.

"I'd like for you to stay around town until we get this saddle business straightened out," Edwards said.

Giff wheeled and went out. He heard someone rise and follow him, but he did not turn to see who it was. He was descending the steps when he heard a voice say sharply from behind him, "Wait, Dixon."

He halted, and waited for the agent's approach. The anger in Welling's face was evident as he hauled up and regarded Giff.

"I want to talk to you."

"You are."

"Not here."

"What's the matter with the saloon?" Giff asked with open malice. "That's where you talk best."

Welling didn't answer, only wheeled and headed downstreet toward the Plains Bar four doors down. Giff followed at his elbow, and they went into the saloon together. A few riders were conversing at the bar, and they looked incuriously at the pair as they entered and took a front corner table.

Defiantly Welling caught the eye of the bartender, called, "Whiskey please," and then sat back in his chair and waited for the bottle and glasses to be brought. Giff toed a chair out and sat down.

Welling had his drink, probably the morning's first because he shuddered a little, then folded his hands on the table, pursed his lips, and settled his stern glance on Giff.

"You made a holy show out of yourself this morning, didn't you?"

Giff only shrugged indifferently.

"Who gave you authority to speak up with that cock and bull story?"

Giff raised his hand and touched his bruised face. "This."

Welling said angrily, "I would like to remind you again that you were hired as a packer and guide only."

"Was I hired to get kicked silly in a dark alley?"

"That was bad luck, but it doesn't change what I said."

"You say too much and you say it in the wrong places," Giff said flatly. "You were here yesterday afternoon bragging about breaking open this case as soon as you had seen a man. All right. Albers is dead."

"You're talking without knowing any facts of the case," Welling said stiffly.

"I know all the facts. Fiske told me." He leaned forward in his chair. "Look," he said flatly. "What did you haul me in here for—to spank me or to fire me? Which is it?"

"To fire you," Welling said levelly.

"Have you talked with Fiske?" Giff asked slowly.

"What about? Firing you? No, that's my own decision."

Giff looked at him wonderingly. Apparently, Fiske had not told him of his resignation. There was something laughable in Welling's pomposity, but also there was something strange in his words. Why was Welling so anxious to get rid of him?

He asked bluntly, "Tell me something, Welling. Answer it straight. Do you want to prove this land swindle against Sebree and Deyo?"

Welling's florid face darkened. "If there is a swindle, yes."

"You don't believe there is?"

"I don't know. There's a dignified way of going about finding out. It has nothing to do with lying under oath and calling names carelessly and baiting influential people, though."

"That's too rough?" Giff asked.

"For a representative of the government, yes. That's why I think it's better for you to find some other work. I'll pay Burton for the saddle you took. I think that ought to square accounts and more between us, don't you?"

Giff heard the saloon door open behind him. He was aware that someone was approaching behind him, and he turned. Gus Traff stood beside him. There was no sleepy malice in Traff's eyes now. He didn't bother to look at Welling, who remained seated, but he regarded Giff with a cold and savage calm.

"I think you're a Sunday man," Traff said coldly. "I don't think you've got the guts to say to my face what you said at the hearing."

Giff's anger was swift and immediate. He rose, reached out, grabbed Welling's bottle of whiskey by its neck, and in a sweeping backhanded motion picked it up from the table and clouted Traff on the side of the jaw. Traff did not even stagger, he simply fell into the adjoining table and made no effort to catch himself as the table legs buckled and caved under him. He rolled over on his side and lay motionless, unconscious.

Welling rose with such haste that his chair tipped over backward. For a brief moment, fright was plain on his loose face. Then he said, "You damn fool! You've probably killed him."

"I meant to."

Giff wheeled and walked out of the saloon, crossed the plankwalk, ducked under the tie rail and headed across the street toward the livery. He knew now that by hitting Traff he had pushed himself toward a final, irrevocable decision.

At the livery office Cass Murray was seated at his desk. He had one foot atop it tying the lace of his farmer's shoe. At sight of Giff, he shook his head in mute wonder. "Well, after that speech to Arnold you won't be needing any horses, will you?"

"I'll need something else first," Giff said. "Have you got a gun?"

Cass lowered his leg, never taking his glance from Giff's face. "Traff or Welling?"

"If it was Welling I would have asked for a stable broom," Giff said.

Cass did not smile. "If it's Traff, you've made a mistake."

"It's my own."

Cass regarded him a silent moment, then said, "You got any Indian in you?"

"About the gun," Giff reminded him.

"Yeah, I got one." Cass reached down and pulled out the lower drawer from which he took an ancient Colt's .44 holstered in a scuffed and scarred shell belt. He laid it on the desk top and asked, "Still working for Welling?"

"He says not," Giff said. He belted on the gun, nodded his thanks, then started for the door. Suddenly, he halted and turned to Cass, his dark face sober. "What's a Sunday man, Cass?"

"He's a man that's a real man only one day of the week, on Sunday. The rest of the week he isn't any man at all. Why?"

The slow smile that came to Dixon's face was not

pleasant. He looked thoughtfully at Cass, said, "No reason," and walked out.

Cass sat a moment after Giff had gone, then, curiosity prodding him, he rose and went out to the street and looked up it. He saw Dixon mount the hotel steps, then vanish. *What's eating him?* Cass wondered.

His attention was attracted to a pair of men hurrying toward the Plains Bar. A third man came out of it on the run, heading for the hotel. It took Cass a few seconds to connect Dixon's strange request for a gun with the saloon across the street; when he did, he moved out into the street and headed unhurriedly for the Plains Bar.

Immediately he entered he saw the crowd of men collected around a figure on the floor. Cass elbowed his way inside the circle and saw Gus Traff stretched out amid the wreckage of a broken table and a smashed chair. Traff was unconscious, and kneeling beside him was a Torreon rider who now looked up in bafflement at another Torreon rider beside him. "It could be broke," the kneeling man said.

Cass felt a solid pleasure at the sight of Traff in this condition and he asked his neighbor, "What happened to him?"

"He got belted with a full bottle of whiskey by that-there packer for the special agent."

Bravo, Cass thought, and then he sighed. *Not to Traff and not that way,* he amended glumly. The bartender broke through the circle, now holding a glass pitcher filled with water. Phlegmatically he poured it on Traff's face and chest. When Traff did not move, the bartender said, "Sure he ain't dead?"

The kneeling puncher said sharply, "Hell, can't you see his chest move? He's breathing." Again the puncher felt gingerly along Traff's right jaw, which was already swollen and beginning to flush.

The beginning of an idea crept into Cass's mind as he watched the puncher. The idea took only seconds to seem really good and then Cass said scornfully to the

puncher, "Go ahead and poke his jaw. Every time
you touch it, you're likely mashing bones."

The puncher glanced truculently at him, and Cass
continued, "Hasn't anyone here thought of Doc Miller?"

The two Torreon punchers glanced at each other.
The services of a doctor for the bruises of a barroom
brawl were seldom required in the circles in which they
moved. The idea appeared to seem daring, but worth
some thought.

Cass prodded, "Well, have you?"

The first puncher looked worriedly down at Traff
and said tentatively, "Maybe we ought to."

This was what Cass was waiting for. He said, "I'll get
him," and turned to elbow his way out through the
crowd.

On the street, Cass really hurried now. Dr. Miller's
office was around the corner two doors, and up a flight
of stairs. When Cass burst into the waiting room, Dr.
Miller, seated in a straight chair with his feet propped
up on an adjoining one, was in idle conversation with
a rancher from the Short Hills. Cass said, "Doc, I've
got to talk to you."

Dr. Miller was a young man, barely thirty, with
short cut hair, a long, aggressive face, and a tall, well-
fleshed indolent body. He came to his feet lazily and
the rancher arose too, saying, "Well, so long, Doc."

Dr. Miller said to Cass, "Will this do or do you want
to see me in the office?"

Cass said, "This'll do," and waited until the rancher
closed the door of the office. Dr. Miller had already
assumed his former position and he eyed Cass curiously
as Cass crossed the room.

"Do you know Gus Traff?" Cass asked and because
he was certain Dr. Miller did, he went on, "Well, your
friend Dixon just belted him across the face with a bottle of whiskey. He's sleeping on the Plains Bar floor."

Dr. Miller said wryly, "The country wouldn't
be lucky enough to have him die." The dislike in his
voice seemed heartfelt to Cass, and Cass asked irrelevantly, "Doc, how honest are you?"

Dr. Miller said warily, "Reasonably. Why?"

"Too honest to pretend a patient's got something that he hasn't got?"

"Certainly."

"How do you fix a broke jaw?" Cass asked, again irrelevantly. He was in a hurry and impatient.

"That's a foolish question. Where's it broke? How could I tell how I'd fix it unless I saw it?"

"Does it hurt to fix it?"

"It hurts to get it; it hurts to fix it; it hurts to have it," Dr. Miller said. Suddenly an alertness came into his eyes and he straightened up. "I see," he said slowly and he gave Cass a brief searching glance, then grinned. "Are you sure it isn't broken?"

"No."

"I think I'll find that it is," Dr. Miller said. He took his coat off the back of his chair, shrugged into it, got his bag from the office and followed Cass down the stairway.

On the plankwalk, he said, "You'd better stay clear of this, Cass."

"Can't I even watch?"

"Part of it." Then he added grimly, "The whole town can watch the rest of it."

At the Plains Bar the crowd of men around Traff gave way for Dr. Miller. He knelt beside the still unconscious Traff, sought for the pulse in his wrist, found it, then gently probed along the bruises on Traff's jaw.

Cass saw him shake his head in discouragement and a slow delight came to Cass. *Don't overdo it, Doc,* Cass thought.

"Is it broke, Doc?" one of the Torreon punchers asked.

"How do I know, man?" Dr. Miller retorted irritably. He looked up at the puncher who had spoken, "Isn't there some place we can take him where I can get to work?"

The puncher addressed looked at the second Torreon rider who said, "What about the hotel?"

Dr. Miller rose, said decisively, "Good. Lend a hand, you men."

Remembering the Doctor's admonition to stay out of this, Cass did not volunteer his help, but he trailed the crowd over to the hotel and watched the five volunteers stagger up the steps under Traff's inert hulk and vanish abovestairs.

He bought a cigar and settled down in a lobby chair to wait. The more he reflected on what he and Dr. Miller plotted, the more the idea delighted him. He hoped passionately that Dr. Miller would crucify Traff, for in some manner Traff had come to symbolize everything Cass and the whole country hated in Torreon. Sebree was too smooth, too remote, too bloodless to nourish real hate; while Traff, the open executor of Sebree's dirty schemes, was a tough, cool bully. Cass had occasion to remember just how tough he was.

The galling memory of that day had been with Cass for five years. Even now he could smell the bitter smoke of his burning stand of wheat that Traff and the Torreon crew had set afire. He remembered how he had run from his shed to the house for a gun and how Traff had ridden him down, his horse knocking him, sprawling, against the cabin. He could even remember the color of the horse Traff rode that day. That wasn't remarkable, for while he had lain in the dust of that hot August day, his arms and legs tied with Traff's lariat, he had time to watch it all—the cabin go up in flames, the sod barn pulled down, his barbed wire fence uprooted, his field ablaze and his homestead wrecked. He hoped Doc Miller would make it long and painful.

When the first of the five men who had remained upstairs to assist Doc came down, Cass prudently left the lobby and went back to the livery office. He had been there only a few minutes when Dr. Miller stepped in the doorway, black bag in hand.

"Was it broken?" Cass asked.

Dr. Miller said solemnly, "There's no sure way of telling. Still a doctor can't afford to assume that it isn't, can he?" He winked, but his sober expression remained. "I managed to get a wire loop around the base of seven of his teeth. The wire must be very tight in order to hold the bones in place—if they are broken, that is! It's extremely uncomfortable," he paused. "The word 'uncomfortable' is a medical understatement for 'painful.' "

"Poor man!" Cass said. "Will he have to wear them long?"

"I believe he will," Dr. Miller said. They looked at each other in what might have been called mutual admiration; then Dr. Miller stepped out.

The five o'clock dimness of the hotel corridor was no help to Fiske in fitting his key into the door. After seconds of fumbling, he found the lock, opened the door, stepped into the room and halted.

Giff Dixon was seated in the armchair across the room, his feet propped up on the window sill. His hat lay on the floor beside him, and the expression with which he looked at Fiske held a certain disappointment.

"Welling with you?" Giff asked.

"No. Come for your money?" Fiske walked across to the table and threw his hat on it, eyeing Dixon quizzically. *How did he get in a locked room?* he wondered, and thought he ought to ask. But there was a kind of quiet balefulness in Dixon's face that checked his question. The young man came to his feet and stared thoughtfully out the window. Either he had not heard Fiske's question or did not intend to answer it.

From under his arm, Fiske took a copy of that day's *Free Press* and threw it on the table. "Seen the paper?"

Dixon half turned to look at him and shook his head.

"The reward notice got in," Fiske said, a grim satisfaction in his voice. "I never thought it could be done."

Dixon wheeled and came slowly across to the table. He put both fisted hands on it and looked levelly at Fiske. "What good will it do, even if you get the April seventeenth copy?"

"Why, I thought you understood that. I thought—"

"What good will it do if it's up to Welling to use it?" Giff demanded insistently.

Fiske understood him then; he only shrugged, but he felt a sardonic appreciation of the younger man's question. "That's not for you to decide."

"Look," Giff said levelly. "You've been the tough uncle to me long enough. If I won't decide, will Welling?"

"He's the Special Agent."

"Is he?" Dixon eyed him coldly. "Or is he scared? Or is he waiting for a bribe from Sebree to call off his investigation? You heard him at the hearing. You heard him crawl, and you heard him turn on me. Now you tell me what he is."

Fiske said wryly, "A man can be a coward and still be reasonably honest."

Dixon shook his head slowly. "Make it plainer than that."

"All right." Fiske thought a moment, reaching for the words to frame his own hard judgment of Welling. "There's more than meets the eye in this, son. Did you know a United States senator is a Torreon stockholder?"

Dixon was listening carefully, and Fiske went on with a fierce distaste in his voice, "Stealing public land is fashionable in the West. There's a lot of land, and the big boys have organized to get their share of it, and more. There are a lot of men who go to church, love their wives and don't cheat at cards who think it's right and proper to cheat the government." He grimaced. "Welling knows that. He knows if he steps on Sebree's toes, it'll be the senator's head that howls. He doesn't like this job. It's too big, and the people are too important. He'd be happy to find a minor error or two in Deyo's records, write a sharp report about the carelessness of land office clerks and go home."

"Then why was he bragging about turning up a big swindle as soon as he saw Albers?"

Fiske grinned. "When you were ten, didn't you whistle when you passed a graveyard at night?"

Dixon straightened up, and gave Fiske a long and searching look. "There's been a murder."

"Welling knows that, and he's preparing to ignore it. That's why he disclaimed responsibility for your talk at the hearing."

Fiske watched Dixon accept that; it took him ten long seconds, and Fiske saw the flaming resentment rise and then fade away in his dark eyes.

"Who gets Sebree? Do you?"

"I'm a surveyor."

"Not Welling, then?"

"Probably not."

"Then who?"

Fiske shrugged, and suddenly he could not hold Dixon's hot glance.

Giff turned then, and walked slowly over to his chair, stooped down and picked up his hat from the carpet. He stood there looking at the hat in his hand, then his glance lifted swiftly to Fiske. "It's a funny thing," he said musingly, "I never earned more than a trail hand's wages in my life. I'm no surveyor, either. But I'm not scared of Traff. Sebree is like any other crook. Deyo is a soft-bellied counterjumper." He paused. "And right is right, and wrong is wrong to me. I wonder what's the matter with me?"

Fiske had no ready answer, and before he could think of one, the door swung open and Welling stepped inside the room. When he saw Dixon, he halted abruptly—too abruptly, for he swayed slightly. He had been at the Plains Bar all afternoon, Fiske knew.

Welling said in a bluff, slurred voice, "What are you doing in here?"

Dixon didn't answer him, only watched him quietly.

"I thought I made it plain that you quit working for me several hours ago. What do you want—money?"

Dixon only shook his head slowly, and Fiske could see the cold contempt for Welling in his somber face.

"Then get out!" Welling said roughly.

Dixon didn't move, didn't speak for long seconds. Then he said quietly, "Suppose you move me out."

Welling came further into the room toward the table, his glance still on Dixon.

"I'll say this again," he said flatly. "You're fired!

You're not working for the Land Office any more. I'll pay for the theft of the saddle. You're through! Now get out!"

Deliberately, Dixon reached in his shirt pocket for his sack of tobacco, and carefully fashioned a cigarette. Welling watched him with a kind of wrathful fascination. Giff licked the edge of his cigarette paper, struck a match with his thumbnail, lighted the cigarette, then looked at Welling.

"I like the job. I think I'll keep it."

It took a moment for his words to sink into Welling's fuddled brain. Then he said pompously, "I don't intend to argue with a camp swamper. I'll see Sheriff Edwards about this." He turned and started for the open door, and Dixon fell in behind him.

"I'll go with you."

Welling paused in his stride as if to speak and then went out, Giff following. Somewhere down the hall, Giff heard a door close, but he paid it no attention. Downstairs, he and Welling crossed the lobby and went out together. They had skirted the stepping block and were almost to the hitch rack in front of Edwards' store when Giff said, "Sure you want to see the sheriff?"

"I said I did."

"Because if you have to see him, I guess I have to see him too. I think maybe I could straighten him out on Albers' death. I think he might be curious as to why you are suppressing Albers' letter to you."

Welling hauled up so abruptly that a puncher who was crossing the street behind them almost bumped into him. The puncher had been whistling idly, tossing a silver dollar in the air and catching it. With no letup in his whistling, he glanced at them incuriously and ducked under the tie rail.

Welling looked sharply at Giff and said, "You're bluffing."

"All right, let's go."

"Look," Welling said wrathfully. "I didn't hire you and I don't have to keep you! I asked Edwards for a chainman and a packer! You're unsatisfactory. Now will you quit this foolishness and go away?"

"No."

"But why?" Welling demanded in exasperation.

"Because you're all primed to run, Welling," Giff said softly. "You've taken a look at the big dog, and your tail's down. As soon as you can pull the cork, you'll crawl back into your bottle of whiskey." He shook his head. "Not while I'm here. And I'm here."

Welling didn't even answer him. He moved onto the plankwalk, and suddenly turned downstreet. He skirted the whistling puncher who apparently had dropped his dollar through a crack in the plankwalk and was on his knees searching for it. Giff walked around the puncher too, without noticing him, and fell in beside Welling. Again they walked silently side by side, ignoring each other.

Surprisingly, when they drew abreast the *Free Press* office, Welling turned in, Giff following. Mary Kincheon came from the print shop at the sound of the door being closed. When she saw Giff, she halted, nodded, and then regarded Welling with a close curiosity.

"Good afternoon, ma'am," Welling said, and touched his hat. "I'd like to place an advertisement in next week's issue."

"You already have one in today's and it isn't paid for," Mary said tartly. "Let's get that settled first. It'll be two dollars."

Her abruptness brought a startled look to Welling's face. He looked blankly at her for a moment, then remembered, and said, "Oh, yes. I'd forgotten that."

He reached in his pocket and pulled out his wallet and handed Mary two silver dollars. As he finished, the door opened behind him, and a puncher stepped into the office. He closed the door and put his back against the wall, as if waiting his turn.

Mary gave him a glance as she went over to the desk and without sitting down, drew paper and pencil toward her, then looked expectantly at Welling. Welling quoted: " 'To whom it may concern, Gifford Dixon, formerly employed by the General Land Office, has been discharged. He has no authority to purchase sup-

plies, sign vouchers or speak for the General Land
Office in any capacity whatsoever.' Sign that, please,
'Vincent X. Welling, Special Agent, General Land
Office.' "

Welling glanced at Giff now and said mildly, "Your
newspaper advertisement gave me the idea. Thanks."
He turned to Mary then and said, "How much will
that be, Miss?"

"Not a penny, because we won't print it," Mary said.
As if to underline her words, she folded the paper,
tore it in quarters, eighths, sixteenths, and then deposited it in the wastebasket.

Welling regarded her with total amazement and for
long seconds he did not speak. "Why won't you print
it?" he asked at last.

"That's a right all newspapers reserve for themselves,
isn't it?"

"Are you the publisher of this newspaper?"

"No. You'll find him over at the billiard table in
Henty's saloon. Go tell him I wouldn't print it. Then
he'll come to me and tell me to print it and I still won't
print it and I still won't get fired."

Welling looked from Mary to Giff and back to Mary.
"What's going on between you two?" he demanded.

"Mostly hard words," Mary said dryly.

"Then why can't I get that printed?"

Mary gave him a searching, thorough stare as if she
were examining something new and distasteful to her.
"Just assume that I don't like the color of your bloodshot eyes. That's reason enough for me."

Welling's face flushed and he glanced quickly at Giff
whose face was expressionless. "Haul her up to the
sheriff's," Giff jibed.

Welling wheeled and tramped out of the office past
the waiting puncher, slamming the door behind him
with the petulance of a child.

Mary said to the puncher, "Something for you?"

"A paper."

"Try the hotel or any of the saloons. We're out."

The puncher nodded, touching his hat and went out.

Mary glanced at Giff, then, "Did I do right?"

Giff was looking at the door, and now his glance shuttled to Mary. "Who's that?"

"I don't know. Why?"

Giff didn't answer. *I've seen him,* he thought, *and where?* but he couldn't place him. Then it came to him. *The fellow who whistled and tossed the coin.* He was the man who had dropped that same coin through the plankwalk. Remembering now, Giff knew that Welling's voice had been raised in anger, so overhearing him would have been easy. He knew with sudden conviction that the puncher had heard every word of his argument with Welling. Furthermore, he had just heard Welling's attempt to fire his chainman publicly.

Standing there, scowling, Giff thought of another thing, too. The hotel room door had been open when they argued. And another door had closed softly as they went into the corridor, Giff remembered now.

Without a word, he turned and tramped out. Looking upstreet, he saw the puncher hurrying up the boardwalk. Increasing his pace, Giff kept the puncher in sight in the late afternoon crowd.

The puncher was in a hurry. Two doors below the Plains Bar, he cut across the road, heading for the hotel. Now Giff moved to a dog trot, so that as he reached the lobby he saw the puncher starting to take to the stairs. At the landing, Giff slowed, and saw the man turn right at the head of the stairs, toward the front of the hotel. Then he lunged up the steps three at a time and was just in time to see the door of the room adjoining Welling's close.

He stood motionless a moment, coming to his decision, then he followed. At the door he paused long enough to lift Cass's gun out, then he softly palmed the knob. The door wasn't locked, and he threw it open, stepping inside.

Traff lay on one the beds, a towel pressed to the side of his swollen face. Sebree sat at the desk chair, listening to the puncher's report. A couple of riders, chairs tilted against the wall, swiveled their heads at his entrance.

In unison, both punchers brought their chairs down to all four legs, and Giff lifted his gun in their direction, "Sit still!"

His glance shuttled to Sebree, and he asked thinly, "What do you think of it?"

Sebree said pleasantly. "I haven't heard it all yet."

"I'll finish it for him," Giff said. "Welling wants to fire me. I'm still working for him. I'll work for him as long as he stays."

"That's interesting, but not very," Sebree murmured.

"One more thing."

Sebree waited.

"They shouldn't have kicked me," Giff said slowly. "That was a mistake. I'll make it a mistake."

Sebree didn't comment, and Giff backed out, closing the door behind him.

As soon as the door was closed, both punchers lunged out of their chairs, headed for it.

"No!" Sebree said sharply. The two halted, and looked sullenly at him. "Go downstairs and wait, all of you."

The three went out, and Sebree made a slow circle of the room, head lowered on his chest. When he hauled up beside the bed, he looked down at Traff and said, "Can you talk, Gus?"

"It hurts like hell to," Traff said in a muffled, dull voice.

Sebree said, almost musingly, "A drunk and a hardcase—and they hate each other. If the drunk shoots the hardcase, that can't be helped, can it, Gus?"

Traff's eyes rolled toward him, and he looked at Sebree for several seconds. "Welling isn't the man to do it."

Sebree smiled, and shook his head once. "No, he isn't. But load him with whiskey some night, and in the morning he'll believe he did."

3

TALTAL WAS a stage stop in the high pines before the last long haul to the pass for Taos. Night was kind to it, for it was a small raffish collection of adobe buildings, and pole corrals and log barns beside the creek. The big building was a hotel of sorts; it served meals that a man could forget in the bar that opened off the dining room, but in the half-dozen shoddy rooms above, sleep was made impossible by the constant rush of the creek whose sound was magnified and thrown back by the steep walls of the narrow canyon in which the hotel was located.

Tonight, as Sebree approached it, he reined in before he crossed the creek, not wanting his horse to announce his presence yet on the noisy planks of the bridge. He saw no horses at the saloon's tie rail, and the up-stage had already passed. But he knew that the nameless fiddle-footed drifters, the shifty riders who traveled the back trails, and the small-time rustlers often stopped at the place for a lone drink or to stay a week. For Sid Bentham, who had looked upon the face of trouble and therefore never invited it, seldom asked questions; the slow-witted Mexican family he employed were incurious and could speak no English.

Sebree had his look at the dim-lit bar and the almost dark dining room, and satisfied, crossed the bridge, tied his horse at the saloon tie rack and climbed the steps. It had been three months since his last visit, he remembered, and thinking of Sarita, Sid's wife, he thought drearily, *She'll be nasty, but it can't be helped.*

He entered the dining room where a fat Mexican woman was wiping off the long oilcloth covered table.

"Where's Sid?" he asked her without bothering with a greeting.

In the fashion of her people, the woman pointed with her chin to the kitchen.

"Get him."

The woman left and Sebree walked through the doorway into the saloon adjoining. It was a comfortable room, low ceilinged and cool. The bar and two oversized circular card tables with their chairs almost filled the room. An overhead kerosene lamp burned dimly. Sebree turned up its wick, then slacked into a chair and idly studied the labels of the whiskey bottles on the back bar. He heard footsteps crossing the dining room and was relieved that they were not a woman's. Sid Bentham came through the doorway, said, "How are you, Grady?" then halted at the end of the bar. He was a spare, clean man past middle age, dressed in townsman's clothes, and his dead white hair parted deep on the side was combed with a barber's neatness. His features were sharp and had once been handsome, but now a cynical weariness was reflected in his dark eyes. "Sarita will be 'long in a minute," he said.

"It's you I want to see, not her."

Wordlessly Bentham turned and went back into the kitchen.

Sebree wondered if Bentham had ever spoken an unnecessary word. He remembered the night in Henty's saloon two years ago when he had caught Bentham dealing a marked deck of cards. Only the two of them had been playing and the game was Black Jack. As Henty's new houseman, Bentham had not yet learned the names and habits of the customers. Sebree had been drinking; Bentham saw it, underestimated his man and took the chance. When Sebree had said suddenly, "Give me that deck," Bentham settled back in his chair, looked blandly at him without any fear at all, and said, "All right, they're marked. Want me to wake Henty?" That was the night that Sebree found a husband for Sarita, who had been his mistress for a year.

He often wondered how Bentham, a townsman at heart, bore the tedium and isolation of this remote spot.

The fact that he was married to another man's woman wouldn't bother him, Sebree knew. It had been an arrangement of convenience and had worked out admirably. Bentham could watch Sarita, and the fact that she was Mrs. Bentham, combined with Sid's earned reputation as a rough man with a gun, kept other men at a distance.

Sid came back now, halted by the bar, and said, "Want a drink?"

"Yes, brandy." Sebree watched Bentham take down two glasses and a bottle and he asked, "How is she?"

"I haven't asked her."

Sebree smiled, but did not comment. Bentham brought the glasses to the table, sat down and poured the brandy. He accepted Sebree's offer of a cigar and both men lit up in silence. If Bentham was curious as to Sebree's mission, he did not show it. That was a quality Sebree admired in a man—that and the ability to be really secretive, which Bentham had also.

When Sebree had sipped his brandy and had his cigar burning evenly, he said, "Sid, you've never told me this, but I took the trouble to find out. You ran with a hardcase crowd over in Beaver County before you came here, didn't you?"

Sid nodded.

"I want a man for a job. He'll kill a man."

Sid's expression did not change; his level glance held Sebree's, and then he asked quietly, "In a fight?"

"No." Even now there was no censure in Bentham's face. Sebree continued, "I don't want a drunken, loud-mouthed gun hand. I want a quiet, sober, middle-aged man whose face you'd forget as soon as you looked away from it. Can you get him?"

Bentham looked at his cigar a long moment, then he nodded. "Jim Archer; but he'll come high."

"How high?"

"I can't say, but I can get him."

Sebree knew that Bentham was planning on keeping at least half of the asking price but that was agreeable to him. He didn't mind this sort of harmless blackmail as long as Bentham's man was reliable, and Sebree knew he would be.

Sebree said, "Send for him, then. I don't want to see him. Tell him to register at the Territory House and wait until somebody gets in touch with him. Tell him to stay sober and talk to nobody. Make it plain to him that he's on his own and that I'll probably place a reward on his head afterward."

A flicker of amusement touched Bentham's cynical eyes and then vanished. "How soon do you want him?"

"Right away." Sebree drew out his wallet and carelessly counted out five hundred dollars in double eagles and shoved them across the table. "Will that be enough?"

Bentham nodded and pocketed the money.

A woman's sullen voice came from the doorway then. "From here, that looks like a lot of money." Both Sebree and Bentham glanced up. Sarita, her shoulder against the door frame, her arms folded across her breast, was watching them. She was a black-haired full-bosomed girl in her middle twenties. From her Mexican mother, she had inherited a dark-eyed sullenness and indolence. From her white father—an Irishman, Sebree had guessed—she had inherited a white, creamy skin that was almost pale. She was, Sebree recognized again, a beautiful woman who, for reasons he could not understand himself, held no attraction for him any more.

He and Sid exchanged a brief glance and then Sebree said, "How long have you been standing there?"

Sarita didn't answer immediately. She was studying Sebree with a cool dislike. "Not long."

"How long?" Sebree insisted.

"I heard you tell Sid to send for him right away. Who?"

Sebree smiled, "I doubt if he'll be young enough to interest you."

"Don't be too sure about that," Sarita said with quiet viciousness. "Anybody who speaks English and is under sixty would look good to me."

Bentham said dryly, "The English isn't necessary."

Sebree laughed openly then, and Sarita straightened up. She came quickly across the room toward them and Bentham, watching her, sighed resignedly.

A wild anger was in Sarita's eyes as she hauled up before Sebree. "Grady, take me out of here! I'm going crazy listening to this damn river day and night! I'm rotting away in this hole! Sid won't talk to me and he won't let me talk even to the stage drivers. Take me out of here!"

"Consult your husband," Sebree said.

Sarita asked wrathfully, "Why do I have to stay here? You never come to see me any more! All I do is wait, and for what—my teeth to drop out?"

"I've been busy," Sebree said evasively.

Sarita looked shrewdly at him. "Has your wife found out about us?"

Sebree laughed. "My dear, she knows all about you."

"Then why can't I go back to town?" Sarita demanded angrily. "Why am I shut up in a dirty shack back in the mountains with an old man for a keeper?"

Sabree said coldly, "I always supposed it was for money."

"And where do I spend it?" Sarita countered.

Sebree sighed wearily and reached for his wallet. "I don't know," he said. "I suppose you can write for anything you want—if you can write."

Sarita raised her hand to hit him. Sebree caught her wrist without rising and said harshly, "Stop this damned nonsense, Sarita!"

"I'm leaving!" Sarita said. "There's no way you can keep me here!"

Sebree let go of her wrist and came to his feet. "That's up to your husband."

Sarita turned swiftly to Bentham, "Can I, Sid?"

Bentham regarded her with a total indifference, "No."

Sebree said, "Why don't you take a trip? Catch the stage out tomorrow and go to Santa Fe. Buy some clothes and wear out a couple of pairs of shoes at fandangos?" He picked up his wallet from the table and emptied it of the remaining double eagles. Picking them up, he extended his hand to Sarita. With a vicious swiftness, she knocked the coins from his hand, turned and ran out of the room.

Sid sighed and rose to pick up the coins. When he had collected them and handed them back to Sebree, he said, "Shall I let her go?"

"I don't care."

"She won't stop running until she's in Kansas City."

"I don't care about that either," Sebree said. Standing, he finished his brandy in one gulp, wiped his mustaches, and said, "Let me know when Archer's in town. Good night, Sid," and moved across the room toward the door.

Sarita, from the kitchen door, heard Sebree go out. Whatever hope she had held of an apology from Grady or even a gesture at reconciliation was gone, and she turned and walked past the big black iron stove to the pump at the sink. She pumped herself a tumbler of water and drank, then stared blankly at the wall. Grady's casual brutality to her tonight was something new, and it signified her total defeat, she knew. With all the bitterness of a perceptive woman, she was aware now that she was simply a piece of goods guarded and sheltered for a man's convenience, and now she was not even desirable.

She remembered with a sharp nostalgia how it had been with Grady up until two years ago. Then she was living in the shabby shack on Corazon's outskirts that her father, a railroad fireman, had left her at his death. In those days, she remembered bitterly, Grady had been wildly jealous of her. It had maddened him to know that she went to dances with ranch hands and town men—affairs his position would not allow him to attend. She suspected, too, that he believed there was something degrading about her surroundings, her taking in laundry to supplement the pittance her father had left, and her careless association with the Mexicans of her mother's blood.

It was this shame, combined with a fear that their relations might be discovered, that had prompted Grady's suggestion of her marriage to Sid Bentham. It would be a marriage in name only, Grady had assured her. It would give her a certain respectability, and his calls on her would have the appearance of a visit to a family. Taltal was a pleasant place, he said, and she would have a woman working for her. The ever-changing stage passengers would keep her amused. And of course, there was the economic side; she would never know want or have to work again, for he had staked Bentham and the place was making money.

There are worse things than work, she thought bitterly. In this brief moment of self-knowledge she saw herself for what she had been—a vain and fuzzy-minded girl without much character who had been flattered that a rich man desired her, but had not been shrewd enough to make that desire pay. Grady had wanted her without any risks attached. His jealousy, his pride and his cynical knowledge that he would some day tire of her had dictated her move to Taltal and her marriage to Sid. Even Grady's fear of his wife's discovering them had been a lie. And now that it was finished, she was married to an old man, a stranger, buried deep in a lonely mountain canyon away from life, from fun, from all affection.

She heard Sid's footsteps in the dining room crossing to the kitchen. She rinsed out the glass and was drying it when Sid came into the kitchen. He had an envelope in his hand, and he gave her a sidelong, indifferent glance on his way to the back door. Then, as if remembering, he halted and said, "He says you can go it you want."

Sarita said nothing, and Sid went out. *Go where?* she thought bitterly. *For what? Who with?* She realized now that she had long since lost her friends.

Her Mexican relatives were still in Corazon, but she found that she had unconsciously acquired from Grady a contempt for their poverty, their ignorance and their shiftlessness. She wouldn't go back to them, but she was shrewdly aware that in spite of her married name of Bentham, she was still a semi-literate Mexican to strangers.

She turned down the lamp over the kitchen table,

then glanced curiously at the back door, wondering what business had taken Sid out into the night, an envelope in his hand. What was it Sid was asking Grady when she halted in the saloon door—*How soon do you want him?* And Grady, counting out the money, had answered, *Right away.* It occurred to her then that Sid's envelope contained a summons for someone.

She moved over to the back door, stepped out into the night. Immediately, the ceaseless noise of the river filled the night with sound. The small adobe shack on the downstream side of the corrals should have been dark and unlit at this hour, for the cook, her hostler husband and their slow-witted son retired not long after dark. There was a lamp lighted in the shack now, and she watched it until the chill of the night made her shiver. Then she saw Julio and Sid, the former carrying a lantern, leave the house and head back for the corrals. Quickly she moved back into the kitchen and began to busy herself adjusting the stove for the night.

Sid came in, gave a civil, "Good night," and moved on into the dining room. She heard his footfalls on the stairs and his slow passage up the corridor to his room in front.

For a moment she stood undecided. She had never interested herself in Sid's business but she had the unspoken conviction, without any proof, that it was not always honest business. On sudden impulse, she blew out the kitchen lamp and stepped outside into the night. She made her way carefully in the dark, skirting the spring wagon which she remembered lay in her path, and halted at the corral. Julio already had the best horse saddled. He was bucking the flap of his bulging saddle bag as she crossed the corral toward him. At the sound of her approach, he turned his head toward her. His habitual expression of surliness, a protest against this grinding work of the station was only surface deep, for he was a lonely, gentle young man. She said in quick Spanish, "Mr. Bentham wants to know if you are carrying enough money, Julio?"

The young man looked at her uncomprehendingly,

then he said, "Isn't this money good where I'm going?"

This was easier than Sarita had hoped for and she asked quickly, "Where is it you are going?"

"A place called Beaver County, Oklahoma—to the east."

"Of course your money is good there. You have it?"

The young man nodded. Sarita said, "Good night," and went back to the hotel.

Pausing in the kitchen, she considered what all this could mean. Grady, through Sid, was summoning a man from Beaver County, Oklahoma, and paying him a surprising sum to come here. She could only speculate on the reason, but remembering the scene in the barroom she was sure of one thing. The reason was secret, and it was important, else Grady would not have been so concerned about how much of his conversation with Sid had been overheard.

A deep malice stirred in her then. Tonight, Grady had turned her loose into a world she really didn't want to reenter. He was finished with her. *But I'm not finished with him,* she thought narrowly. Maybe, by waiting and watching, she could learn the reason behind Grady's strange summons of a stranger from Oklahoma. Once she knew the reason, perhaps she could use it to hurt him.

Giff finished the diamond hitch on the pack mules, and as he moved toward the livery, he glanced at the three saddled horses tied to the corral pole. The dun would be Welling's, he decided; since Welling was paying the bill, he would get the best horse. At the office, he paused in the doorway. Cass Murray had a saddle atop his desk and was reworking the laces on a stirrup.

"Where is he? At the Plains Bar?" Giff asked.

Cass nodded. "He was waiting on the doorstep when Harvey opened up. Have you got anything on the mule that gurgles?"

"That's what he'll be buying now."

Cass straightened up and placed a sober regard on Giff. "I wish he was starting his resurvey somewhere besides Torreon."

"What's the difference?"

"Plenty, and you know it. You watch yourself, hear me?"

Giff raised his hand in mild salute, said, "See you in a week," and moved out of the runway, heading for the Plains Bar. Welling's sudden decision of last night to take to the field for a resurvey of some of Torreon's acquired homesteads still surprised him. He suspected that his own goadings, Fiske's contemptuous silence and a lot of whiskey had prodded Welling into this sudden move against Torreon. It was a decision Welling was probably regretting at the moment, but one it was too late to retract now. And it was of small significance in the big fight against Sebree, Giff knew. It was a sort of tentative pecking at the edge of the swindle; a laborious and quibbling routine of Welling's attempting to find out from reluctant and lying witnesses if homestead requirements had been satisfied. Giff knew it was Welling's tentative show of authority, a kind of timid testing of Sebree's power.

Stepping into the saloon, he saw Welling downing his drink while Fiske watched idly. The saddlebag on the bar beside Welling had twin telltale bulges that Giff knew would be his carefully rationed sustenance of whiskey for the next few days.

At the sight of Giff, they pulled away from the bar and the three of them walked in silence to the livery. For the first hour their talk was sparse, and Welling joined in none of it. He was still brooding, Giff guessed, on his failure to fire his surveyor's chainman, and Giff wondered if he had discussed it with Fiske. Giff was aware that Welling was ignoring him, and he knew that Mary Kincheon's action yesterday was still smarting.

The country north of Corazon was a gently rolling, almost treeless plain, the wagon road running string straight along the very tips of the cedar-stippled foothills. Some time in midmorning they passed a crossroads adobe store and watered their horses at a rusty tank at the base of a clattering windmill. Beyond the store and still north was the first of the Torreon fence. They traveled alongside it for four miles before they

came to the first gate and turned in. Afterward they
moved across Torreon range cutting northeast over an
ocean of grass that held hundreds of fat cattle. Past
midday they came to a seep where Welling had decided the resurvey was to start. The seep, which was
announced from a distance away by the paler green of
cottonwood foliage, lay beneath a limestone outcrop
thrusting a few feet higher than the surrounding country. At the bottom of a small depression stumpy wil-
lows matted the bog created by the small stream as it
flowed east for a hundred yards and then vanished; a
scattering of old cottonwoods surrounded it.

While Fiske unrolled his plat and weighted it with
stones before studying it, Giff unloaded the pack horse,
unsaddled the other mounts and turned them loose,
and made camp. Afterward, Fiske helped him put up
the Sibley tent and stake down a wing of the tarp to
serve as a windbreak for the reading of Fiske's maps.
Welling rode up to the limestone outcrop to locate the
monument that would be the corner for the new survey.

By the time he had returned and turned his horse
loose to graze, Giff had broken out the sandwiches the
hotel had provided for their midday meal, and Fiske
had begun to eat. His mouth full, Fiske nodded to the
limestone outcrop and asked Welling, "Did you see
any buildings from there, Vince?"

"There's an abandoned dugout over the ridge. The
roof's caved in, and it's likely full of snakes." Welling
answered sullenly.

Fiske snorted, "Value about ten dollars, I suppose." He shook his head. Giff, remembering last night's
discussion with Fiske, recalled the old surveyor's prediction. It had concerned what Fiske guessed they would
find at the beginning of the resurvey of homesteads
acquired by Torreon. There was a pattern, Fiske had
said, in all these homestead frauds instigated by cattle-
men. The required improvements were never made on
the property, just as the six-month residence require-
ment was ignored. So long as perjury on the part of the
entryman's witnesses was a custom accepted by the
Land Office, the pattern still held. One of Sebree's

riders had "homesteaded" this waterhole, and for his cheerful dishonesty and for the casual perjury of his two witnesses, he was probably rewarded with a bottle of whiskey or an extra day in town. Fiske had predicted they would find no improvements and no indication of residence, and Welling's facts seemed to be bearing him out.

Welling, already sore from the morning's unaccustomed ride, stifled a sigh as he sat down and reached for his sandwich. The three of them heard the sound of approaching riders at the same time.

Giff rose first, sandwich in hand, and saw the two riders who had come up behind the tent. They were moving through the grouped horses grazing around the seep and the first rider had a rifle across his saddle. Giff glanced briefly at Welling. Fiske was watching him too with a mild accusation so that Welling said sullenly, "I didn't see them."

One rider, a Mexican, dropped back so that he was between the tent and the survey party's horses. The man with the rifle reined in by the tarp, contriving to pull in his horse so that the rifle, still resting on the pommel, covered the three men afoot.

Welling, sandwich in hand, gestured to the food on the ground and said affably, " 'Light and eat."

Giff was watching the rider and he didn't like what he saw. The man's clothes were almost tatters and he had the hungry half-mean look of an overworked rider whose staggering amount of labor, whose unwavering loyalty and whose life are hired for a dollar a day by the big cattle companies.

"Know where you are?" the man asked.

"Torreon, aren't we?" Welling said.

The rider dipped his head briefly in assent. "This is private land. Get off it."

Welling's quick smile seemed not to betray any uneasiness, "We're Land Office men on a resurvey."

"Not here you aren't. You're trespassers."

Welling's voice held a quiet confidence as he said, "My friend, I can bring the sheriff with me, only it's a long ride to get him. Maybe I had better put it this way. If I'm barred from resurveying this land, I'll recommend all patents granted be canceled and the land will revert to the public domain."

The rider moved his rifle until it pointed at Welling. "You take that up with the boss. Now take your left hand—left I said—and lift your gun out and throw it over the tent."

Only then did Welling seem to realize that his authority meant nothing here and now. He glanced at Fiske in rising anger and bafflement and then shuttled his gaze to the rider.

The man said quietly, "I don't fool," and lifted the rifle slowly to his shoulder.

"All right, all right," Welling said hastily, and did as he was bid. The rider turned his attention to Fiske then and said, "You do the same."

"I don't pack one," Fiske said.

The rider looked at Giff now, "You, too."

"The hell with you," Giff said quietly.

The rifle began to rise again. Giff looked up and along the barrel into the rider's eye and a wild stubbornness was in him.

"Once more. Throw your gun away."

Giff didn't move. It was Welling, prodded by fright, who moved over to Giff, yanked the gun from the waistband of his pants and threw it hastily over the tent as if it were red hot.

The rifle slacked back to the pommel and the rider said levelly, "There's a gate southwest about six miles. Your horses will be tied to it. Tomorrow you can pick up this stuff there too." He gave Giff a hard, lingering stare of almost respectful curiosity before he turned his head and signaled to the Mexican. Pulling his mount around he gave Welling's horse a cut across the rump with his rope and then, half circling the other horses and whistling shrilly, the pair of them pushed the animals up over the rim of the depression and were out of sight.

Fiske and Welling glanced briefly at each other, then both looked at Giff. "I don't know why I didn't let him shoot you," Welling said angrily.

"I know why. You were scared." Giff said thinly. "By a bluff."

The color crept into Welling's loose face and he said sardonically, "That's a second guess you can afford, now he's gone."

"He was hazing you and you took it."

Welling glanced at Fiske in appeal. "You think so, Bill?"

Fiske made a wry face and thumbed his derby off his forehead. "I hate to admit it, but I think he was."

Welling considered this under Giff's hot gaze. Giff said, "Sebree put him up to it. You're afoot with a long hike ahead of you. The boys in Henty's will be laughing about it tonight."

Welling's eyes held a deep hatred as he looked at Giff. Fiske, sourly regarding the sandwich he still held in his hand, said, "Did he say six miles?"

Giff said, "It's eight."

"He said six," Welling countered flatly.

Giff swiveled his head to look at Welling. His face was stiff, and still held the dregs of anger. "I'm talking about the distance to the ranch, not the fence."

Welling didn't answer for a moment. "What are you going to do? Complain to Sebree?" he asked with heavy irony.

"In my own way," Giff agreed quietly. "If you aim to stay in this country even another week, you'll come too."

Welling didn't answer him. He turned and walked around the tent and behind it, and Giff heard him pick up the guns. Giff surprised Fiske watching him and he said truculently, "Well?"

"Not my department," Fiske said.

With the two guns in his fist, Welling returned to Giff and handed him Cass's battered Colt. Avoiding the questioning look in Giff's eyes, Welling glanced down at the gun he was holstering and said, "I think we can settle this another way. When Edwards . . ."

Giff didn't wait for any more. He turned and headed south, climbing up and out of the depression. He had walked perhaps fifty yards when Welling called, "Hold on! I'll come with you."

Giff waited. When Welling caught up with him, he started out again without speaking. He knew Welling had no heart for this, and that Fiske's tacit approval of Giff's move had pushed him to his reluctant decision. Giff's instinct now was to send him back, even though he had taunted him into coming. But he would not do it, he knew; for he had spoken the truth when he told Welling the whole countryside would know before night that the Land Office Special Agent was a sorry man who could be pushed and crowded and eventually neutralized. Oddly, Giff cared about that, and he knew what he was about to do had to be done if Welling's investigation were not to collapse.

Since they were both wearing cowman's half boots, Giff anticipated complaints from Welling during the long afternoon. But the fitful wind pressing at their backs, pushing down the grass ahead of them in uneven rhythm across the limitless plains, made talk difficult and Welling held stubbornly to silence. By unspoken agreement they gave occasional bands of cattle a wide detour, since a man afoot was considered legitimate game by these half wild beeves. Once in late afternoon they saw far ahead of them a pair of riders heading in the direction of Torreon. At Giff's command, Welling flattened out alongside him in the grass until the riders were out of sight.

They saw the first trees of Torreon far distant in the early evening. As they drew closer, Giff saw that Torreon headquarters was built in the shallow timbered valley of a wide stream. The house itself was set in a park of rolling lawn and isolated tremendous cottonwoods. It was built of huge timbers, the main part, three stories high, flanked by long wings of stone construction. The carriage house and stables separated the big house from the working part of the ranch.

Beyond them was a long single-story adobe which Giff decided was the combination cookshack and bunkhouse. It was set in a grassless area of scuffed and hardpacked ground that stretched to the tangle of barns, sheds and pole corrals to the east. The first lamps, lighted against the twilight, were burning in the big house. As Giff listened, he could hear the cook's triangle summoning the ranch hands to supper, and at this distance, he could make out men moving from the barns and corrals toward the isolated cookshack.

He saw Welling was watching him with an expression of helplessness and distaste on his face. In order to reach the cookshack without alarming the main house, they would have to make a wide half-circle and Giff picked out his point of approach before he started out. A half hour later, they halted at the corner of a big wagon shed after crossing the horse pasture to the east of the ranch buildings. Giff was waiting for a ranch dog to pick them up in the twilight, but it seemed their coming had gone unnoticed except by a scattering of incurious horses in the pasture.

Ahead of him and across a wide expanse of barn lot, he could see the cookshack, its door open. Lamps were lighted inside and he could even see one rider, his back to the door, industriously attacking his supper. He sensed Welling's aching uneasiness, but he ignored him as he set out for the cookshack.

Welling caught up with him and said hurriedly in a low voice, "I don't like this. They'll all be in there. What do you want me to do?"

"You've got a gun. Stand them off," Giff said. As an afterthought, he drew his own gun and wordlessly passed it over to Welling. He did not want to look at the man, and he had a dismal conviction that Welling wouldn't back up his play.

This was gone from his mind when he took the one step up to the cookshack door, moved across the sill and halted. There were perhaps fifteen men at the big table which was not nearly full, and only a few of them faced the door; the majority had their backs to the door and were seated near the kitchen end of the table.

Almost immediately Giff spotted the tough hungry-looking rider who had set them afoot; he was seated two places from the kitchen door and had his head inches above his plate, wolfing his food. Giff's brief sidelong glance at Welling revealed him standing, both guns leveled, in the doorway with a kind of scared determination in his posture.

Then one of the riders glanced up and saw them. He half rose as Giff said in an iron voice, "Sit down!"

His sudden command, startling in the silence, turned the heads of every crew member toward him. The hungry-looking rider looked up, fork raised halfway to his mouth. Giff took two running steps toward the table, put a foot on the bench, and dived across the table at him. The man already had one leg over the bench and was rising when Giff crashed into him. The rider went over on his side, Giff on top of him, his legs dragging the tin plate of bread off the table. Its clank followed the crash of the two bodies on the floor by seconds.

The men facing Welling scrambled off the bench, out of the way, as Giff and the rider came erect at the same moment.

The rider backed up a step to get set, but Giff was on him. With the tactics of a standard barroom brawler, the man lowered his head, his arms windmilling, and tried to charge. Giff's hook to his face was so swift and vicious that, still moving forward, the man was half turned by the blow and his upper body sprawled on the table.

The rider's hand closed on a heavy stoneware platter and he came off the table with it in his hand in a back-handed sweeping side swipe. Giff saw it too late to evade it; he raised his elbow and ducked his head against it as the platter hit his forearm and caromed off it into the wall. He could hear the shouts of the crew now. Since he was still fighting only one man, he supposed that Welling was successfully standing off the others. How long he could continue to do so, Giff didn't know, and he thought, *Make it quick.*

Now that the rider had named his own kind of fight, Giff moved in against him, lifting his knee into the rider's belly. The man's grunt could be heard above every sound in the room. He wrapped both arms around Giff's midriff, clinging desperately to him while he fought for breath. Giff stepped back, braced himself, and with a savage wrench of his upper body, broke the man's grip. Then he heaved the rider away from him upright, and swung. The blow straightened the rider totally erect. Giff got one brief glance at the man's tortured face before he smashed his fist into it. The rider back-pedaled, fighting for balance, through the door leading into the kitchen. He grabbed wildly at the door frame but his momentum tore his hold loose.

Dimly, Giff heard the roar of the crew, followed by the crash of a gun shot and Welling's voice in a wild yell, "Stand away from him!"

On the heel of Welling's yell, the rider crashed to the floor. Giff lunged at him, doubling his knees under him, and landed heavily on the rider's chest. He heard the wind driven from his lungs in a great tortured sigh. Giff had rolled off the rider and was on his knees. Now he crawled back to him, balled up the man's shirt in his fist and rose, yanking the rider erect. Balancing him, he swung with all his might at the man's face. He saw him teeter backward, hit the corner of the big stove, spin around drunkenly, and fall face first into the wall which held a rack of iron skillets. The force of his body crashing into the wall jarred the skillets off their hooks and they rained down on his unconscious form as it slumped to the floor.

Giff stumbled to the nearest wall and leaned against it, dragging great gusts of air into his heaving lungs. He was aware that his back was exposed and he wheeled as fast as he could, expecting the crew to ignore Welling and rush him. Instead, he saw that Welling had moved around the table and into the kitchen doorway and, back to him, was still holding them off. Unsteadily, Giff shouldered past Welling and confronted the Torreon crew. He reached out and took one of Welling's guns and pointed it at the nearest Torreon hand. "You come out with me and saddle up three horses," Giff said. "The rest of you stay set."

The rider looked first at the gun, then at Giff's hard face, then turned to go out. The crew broke for him. Gun leveled at the man's back, Giff followed. Suddenly, the man halted so abruptly that Giff bumped into him; he was looking across the room and Giff looked too. In the bunkhouse doorway stood a woman.

She was perhaps forty, Giff judged, although her thin autocratic face held a pain-ravaged sternness that made her seem older. Under her right arm was a crutch on which she leaned, her upper body half twisted into it. Her dress was a dead black color and long-sleeved. Her hair, of an auburn color, was so thick as to be almost unruly and she wore it off her neck, coiled carelessly on top of her head. "Who was shooting?" she demanded coldly.

Giff stepped from behind the rider. "I was," he said. "I'll probably shoot again, too."

The woman looked levelly at him and said, "I forbid you to. There is no gunfire allowed at Torreon. Any man who works here should know that."

Giff's voice was dry. "I don't work here, and unless I get three horses saddled right now, you'll likely hear more shooting."

The woman frowned, "Who are you?"

"It doesn't matter," Giff said flatly. "A couple of Torreon hands set three of us afoot this afternoon. I've come for our horses. Since they're not here, I'll take three of yours."

"You're working for the Land Office." It was a statement, rather than a question and Giff nodded. "I'm Mrs. Sebree. Please come to the house with me."

Giff said quietly, "As soon as I have our horses."

Mrs. Sebree said to the crew, "Where are they?"

There was a moment of silence and then a man cleared his throat and said, "Tied to the west gate."

"Get them. Meanwhile give this man as many of our horses as you drove away." Without further words Mrs. Sebree turned and stepped out into the evening. Welling warily circled the table, his gun held at his side, and Giff started after him. He saw his hat on the floor and said flatly to the closest man, "Pick it up." The man obeyed and handed it to him, and afterward he holstered the gun, circled the table and went out.

Mrs. Sebree was waiting outside for them. She asked, "Which one of you is the special agent?"

Welling cleared his throat and said, "I am, Mrs. Sebree." Already his voice held its old note of affability.

Mrs. Sebree said, "Then you'll want to stay here and make sure your horses are satisfactory. There won't be any more trouble, I assure you. Mr. Dixon, please come with me."

It was not quite rudeness, but her point was plain enough. It was Giff she wanted to see, not Welling, and he was excused. She turned then and walked toward the carriage house. Surprisingly, she moved at a normal pace in spite of her limp, and Giff walked beside her in silence. Passing the carriage house, they achieved a gravel driveway. Here Mrs. Sebree rested a moment and Giff unsuccessfully tried to read her thoughts in the lowering darkness. Mrs. Sebree asked abruptly, "Did I hurt that man's feelings?"

"Everyone hurts his feelings."

Mrs. Sebree laughed quietly and started off up the drive toward the big house. At the wide steps of the main house, Giff held out his arm to her. She said, "Thank you, but I do this by myself."

Once on the long veranda, she turned toward a cluster of chairs, halted before one, slipped the crutch from under her arm and sat down. She indicated the chair next to her and Giff, removing his hat, also sat down.

She said, "I would offer you supper but I don't think you are in the mood to accept it from Torreon."

"No, ma'am."

Mrs. Sebree leaned forward, "Tell me, what is it you plan for us?"

"No, ma'am."

Mrs. Sebree was silent a long moment. "You're the man who clouted Gus Traff with the bottle, aren't you?"

Giff said he was. He felt a stiff wariness in talking with this woman. His skinned knuckles were smarting now, and the bones in his hands ached. He felt both irritable and impatient, and only an uneasy politeness kept him seated. The woman might have been holding him for Sebree to punish, or she might only have an invalid's unspoken need for dominating a well person. Giff didn't know which, but instinct told him that he should be out of here, and soon.

Mrs. Sebree said abruptly, "I have been trying for the last ten days to think of how I could help the government trap Grady. I don't think there is any way."

The strangeness of her words held Giff mute. He wondered if he had understood her. She had spoken as casually as if she were discussing the weather. Then he picked the flaw in her statement. "Ten days?" he asked. "The special agent hasn't been here that long."

"Perhaps I should have said, ever since I heard an agent was coming." She hesitated. "Grady's guilty, you know; so is Deyo and so is Kearie. So, too, are all the men behind Torreon, from Senator Warrenrode down through Modesto Salazar to that sniveling old Judge Arnold. It touches some of the biggest names in the Territory."

"Strange you should say so," Giff murmured.

"Why strange? I'm an honest person and no honest person likes Grady."

"Does he discuss business with you?"

"None of it. All I know is what I pick up. Such as, for instance, the reward notice for last year's April seventeenth issue of the *Free Press*. I can guess why that is valuable to you."

Giff said nothing.

"You'll never find it, of course. Perry Albers had it, didn't he?"

Still Giff said nothing.

Mrs. Sebree said bitterly, "I suppose it's difficult for you to trust me."

Giff moved uneasily in his chair but did not speak. There was nothing for him to say.

Mrs. Sebree went on, "Maybe there's something I could tell you. I don't know if it's worth anything. There's a stage stop on the way to Taos called Taltal. It's up in the mountains. Grady keeps a girl up there and her name is Mrs. Bentham. Maybe she could help you."

Giff considered this. "But would she?"

"Of course, any woman who ever had anything to do with Grady turns on him willingly. I think it's time she did."

Giff stood up. "I'll remember that. Thank you. Good night, Mrs. Sebree."

He turned and had taken a step when Mrs. Sebree said, "There's something else you might be interested in. Grady is afraid of Mary Kincheon. Now, good night, Mr. Dixon."

4

WHEN SHERIFF Edwards mounted the balcony which held the business office of his store, it was midmorning. He spoke pleasantly to Arthur Miles, his bookkeeper, who was seated on the high stool before the slanted desk that held an open ledger. Miles was a dry frail man, past middle age and, because he had gambled away the business that Edwards took over from him, he was deeply sensitive to Edwards' treatment of him. The sheriff knew this and he made it a point to be unfailingly kind and courteous with the man.

With the county work, much of which rested in the hands of his deputies, out of the way for the day, Edwards looked over the balcony rail at the bulging shelves and counters and felt at home. The sheriff's duty was a chore he did not relish; he was a merchant down to his very bones.

By the time Edwards was ready to sit down at his desk, Miles had already left a stack of invoices on top of it and returned to his desk. Edwards seated himself and immediately saw the copy of the *Free Press* which he had abandoned the night before when he closed the store. His curiosity of last night was still with him. He bent down and again read the reward notice for a copy of the April seventeenth *Free Press* and again speculated on its meaning. He supposed it had something to do with the land office records and their publication, but just why any printed matter of public knowledge was worth fifty dollars to Welling he did not understand.

He was certain that in the store's files was a copy of the April seventeenth *Free Press* of last year. As

**Enjoy the Best
of the World's Bestselling
Frontier Storyteller in...**

THE
LOUIS L'AMOUR
COLLECTION

**Savor <u>Silver Canyon</u> in this new hardcover
collector's edition free for 10 days.**

At last, a top-quality, hardcover edition of the
best frontier fiction of Louis L'Amour. Beautifully
produced books with hand-tooled covers, gold-
leaf stamping, and double-sewn bindings.

Reading and rereading these books will give
you hours of satisfaction. These are works of
lasting pleasure. Books you'll be proud to pass
on to your children.

MEMO FROM LOUIS L'AMOUR

Dear Reader:

Over the years, many people have asked me when a first-rate hardcover collection of my books would become available. Now the people at Bantam Books have made that hope a reality. They've put together a collection of which I am very proud. Fine bindings, handsome design, and a price which I'm pleased to say makes these books an affordable addition to almost everyone's permanent library.

Bantam Books has so much faith in this series that they're making what seems to me is an extraordinary offer. They'll send you <u>Silver Canyon</u>, on a 10-day, free examination basis. Plus they'll send you a free copy of my new Calendar.

Even if you decide for any reason whatever to return <u>Silver Canyon</u>, you may keep the Calendar free of charge and without obligation. Personally, I think you'll be delighted with <u>Silver Canyon</u> and the other volumes in this series.

Sincerely,

Louis L'Amour

Louis L'Amour

P.S. They tell me supplies of the Calendar are limited, so you should order now.

Take Advantage Today of This No-Risk, No-Obligation Offer

You'll enjoy these features:

- An heirloom-quality edition

- An affordable price

- Gripping stories of action and adventure

- A $6.95 calendar yours free while supplies last just for examining <u>Silver Canyon</u>

- No minimum purchase; no obligation to purchase even one volume.

Pre-Publication Reservation

( ) YES! Please send me the new collector's edition of <u>Silver Canyon</u> for a 10-day free examination upon publication, along with my free Louis L'Amour Calendar, and enter my subscription to <u>The Louis L'Amour Collection</u>. If I decide to keep <u>Silver Canyon</u>, I will pay $7.95 plus shipping and handling. I will then receive additional volumes in the Collection at the rate of one volume per month on a fully returnable, 10-day, free-examination basis. There is no minimum number of books I must buy, and I may cancel my subscription at any time.

05066

If I decide to return <u>Silver Canyon</u>, I will return the book within 10 days, my subscription to <u>The Louis L'Amour Collection</u> will expire, and I will have no additional obligation. The Calendar is mine to keep in any case.

( ) I would prefer the deluxe edition, bound in genuine leather, to be billed at only $24.95 plus shipping and handling.

05074

Name _____

Address _____

City _____ State _____ Zip _____

This offer is good for a limited time only. Supplies of calendar are limited.   I

Detach and Mail Today.

BUSINESS REPLY MAIL

FIRST CLASS   PERMIT NO. **2154**   HICKSVILLE, N.Y.

POSTAGE WILL BE PAID BY

THE LOUIS L'AMOUR COLLECTION

BANTAM BOOKS
P.O. BOX 956
HICKSVILLE, NEW YORK 11801

a careful businessman, he kept a copy of all the store's advertising in the *Free Press* and of their dodgers and throwaways. This system was several years old and it served as a general price index for the products of all the merchants in the town. It both amused and instructed him to see how the cost of goods fluctuated over the years.

The April seventeenth issue of a year ago was undoubtedly stacked away neatly in a corner of the basement set aside for old records, but before he dug out that certain issue and produced it for Welling, he must know to what uses it would be put. He considered that only simple caution, for he was remembering the perjured evidence which Dixon, a land office employee, had retracted under oath at the hearing. Grady Sebree and Torreon were involved in this investigation in some manner, Edwards felt. Before risking possible offense to them, Edwards intended to learn just how they were involved. He would ask Welling today, he thought—and then he remembered that Welling, Fiske and Dixon were all out on a resurvey of some Torreon holdings. It would have to wait.

He was aware with a mild irritation that Miles was standing behind his chair. He detested the silent, furtive way in which Miles moved, and had often thought of belling the cat by giving Miles all the keys to the store and insisting that he wear them on a watch chain across his shabby vest.

"Have you gone over those invoices, Mr. Edwards?" Miles asked. He never referred to Edwards' title of sheriff. An elected county official in Miles's book was something beneath his recognition.

Edwards reached for the invoices and said, "No, Arthur, I'm late on everything this morning," and he promptly forgot the files of the *Free Press*.

Arthur Miles, however, did not. He too had seen the reward item in yesterday's paper, and it had been in his mind half the night and all of the morning. Because Edwards entrusted the filing of all records to him, it was natural that he should remember the basement files—and the fifty dollars reward made it impossible for him to forget it. He was aware of Edwards' interest in it too, and as he worked that morning, he wondered if his employer would speak of it. Sometimes in the late morning Edwards put the newspaper containing the reward notice in the filing drawer, and Miles breathed easier. He was reasonably certain that Edwards, busy with store affairs and with outside interests, had either forgotten it or would forget it.

During the noon hour, Miles, who got off at one o'clock for his midday meal, was relatively alone in the store. One of the clerks, always the youngest, remained downstairs while he *the oldest,* he thought bitterly, kept watch over the records so that no pricing mistakes could happen.

Today, after Edwards had picked up his hat and gone across to the Territory House, Miles descended from the balcony, turned toward the rear of the store and went down into the basement. It was a long dark room, lit only be one dirty basement window on the side street, but he made his way unerringly toward the far front corner where the records were stored. Here he lighted a lamp in a wall bracket, then moved over toward the high stack of *Free Press*es. The April seventeenth issue of the newspaper he found easily, and simple curiosity prodded him into spreading it out on the waisthigh stack of wash tubs beneath the lamp and opening it.

He could see nothing relating to land office business in its news columns, and its advertising columns carried the usual final proof notices required of homesteaders. After noting that Cassel's Hardware in Las Vegas, as of a year ago, was underselling them on cedar fence posts, he folded the paper under his arm and went upstairs.

He smiled without humor at the thought that Edwards, even if he suspected him of the theft would never mention it. Edwards' unfailing tact and consideration for him were a source of malicious and secret delight to Miles. Ever since Edwards had bought the store from Henty, to whom Miles had lost it gambling, Miles's air of humble pride, of sensitivity to his failure had worked a small magic in his relations with Edwards. It was a coin he spent freely, aware that Edwards was too gentle to protest.

Back at his desk he slipped the paper into the drawer and resumed his work. If he had thought about it, which he did not, he would have seen no shame in taking a few cents' worth of stale newsprint and turning it in for fifty dollas. Some day his luck would turn at Henty's monte game; maybe this was the stake that would turn it. All he needed was one run of luck, just one.

When his day's work was done at six, he fussed around until Edwards said, "Be sure the night latch is on, Arthur. I'm leaving. Good night."

When Edwards had gone, Miles turned down the night lamp, then unbuttoned his vest, placed the newspaper against his body, and rebuttoned his vest. Then he closed the store and went down four doors to the Plains Bar where he bought himself his usual six o'clock glass of whiskey. Afterward he crossed to the Territory House, took his customary place at a side table in the dining room, and selected as usual the cheapest meal on the menu. Essentially a friendless man, he did not need company and did not miss it. After finishing his deliberate supper, he went out into the lobby, halted at the desk, nodded good evening to the clerk—a man as old as himself, whose name he had never bothered to learn—and asked, "What's the number of Mr. Welling's room?"

"Number two," the clerk replied. "He isn't in, though."

"When will he be?"

"Can't say. I understand they're all out on a resurvey."

A kind of distress clouded Miles's sallow face. He wanted this done with immediately, since there was always the risk that Edwards would discover this certain copy missing from the files. Besides, Henty's monte table was waiting.

The clerk, seeing Miles's disappointment, eyed him closely. "Is it about the reward?" he asked.

Miles glanced at him uneasily, and uneasily nodded. "After a fashion, yes." Unthinkingly, he brought his hand to his chest to feel the newspaper under his vest. Its muted crinkle was nevertheless distinct enough so that the clerk looked down at his vest. Then the clerk's glance rose swiftly to Miles's face. "Would you want to leave it in the room?" he asked.

Miles said hurriedly, "No! No! I just wanted to talk with him." He turned and beat a swift retreat to the street. *I handled that badly,* he thought irritably. *He'll tell Edwards about me.*

He halted then on the boardwalk to think this out. Why should the clerk tell Edwards? What was so strange about a man having a copy of a wanted newspaper that the clerk would even remember it or think it unusual enough to mention? *Nothing, of course.* He'd let his silly feeling of guilt stampede him. The thing to do was wait until Welling returned to town, show him the paper and explain that he found it rummaging around his attic. Edwards be damned!

The clerk waited only until Miles was out of sight, then he rounded the corner of his desk and hurried over to the dining room doorway. Scanning the room, he did not see the man he was looking for, and wheeling, he hurried up the stairs, turned right and knocked on the door of room number one, Torreon's room.

There was no answer, and thoughtfully, he retraced his steps to the lobby.

Corazon's traffic was at its highest just before the supper hour and Welling was breasting it with a vast impatience. Giff, leading the pack mule in the rear, reined in at the hotel stepping block just as Welling and Fiske were dismounting. The long twelve-hour day they had put in had told upon Fiske. He looked at his horse with a red-eyed irritability and then his glance shuttled up to Giff.

"I'd kick him in the belly if I didn't figure I'd have to ride him again," he said. He looked over at Welling, "This time I'll buy you a drink, Vince." Again his glance touched Giff. "Come on over to the Plains Bar when you're done, Giff."

Giff nodded and stepped stiffly out of the saddle as Fiske and Welling cut across the street toward the saloon. He unpacked the mule, lugged his gear through the lobby and halted at the desk. "Did anyone show up looking for Welling?" he asked the clerk.

The old man eyed him blandly and said, "Nope, nobody."

Climbing the stairs, Giff deposited the gear in Welling's room, then descended and took the animals back to the livery corral.

The day largely had been a futile one of riding from one Torreon line camp to another, taking affidavits— sullenly given by Torreon hands—as to their knowledge of the disputed homesteads. More often than not, the Torreon riders, warned of their coming, had disappeared, so that Welling had uncovered little of value. It didn't matter anyway, Giff had decided. This resurveying and taking of affidavits was only marking time; the real evidence they had to have would be in the missing newspaper, and it had not shown up yet.

He turned the mounts over to the livery hostler and on his way to the street checked to see if Cass had come in. He had not, and Giff knew he was tending his garden. The office was empty and he moved on toward the Plains Bar where Welling and Fiske awaited him. He knew Welling would be happy to be close to whiskey again; he had been without it a day and his nerves were already ragged.

The brawl at Torreon had had a peculiar effect on Welling. It had saddled him with a spurious authority and reputation he knew he could not maintain. It had pushed him to a decision he was not ready to face, and these last two days he had been apathetic and morose. He had declared against Sebree, but his heart was not in it, and Giff knew that Welling held him accountable.

The Plains Bar was crowded and most of the gambling tables were filled. Giff spotted Welling and Fiske, a half-empty bottle of whiskey between them, seated at one of the far tables. Fiske had lighted up a cigar and was comfortably reading an old newspaper. Welling, his face already flushed with many quick whiskies, was idly toying with a cigar from the handful lying on the table between them. Giff came up and settled into the chair next to Fiske, who wordlessly passed over the bottle and a glass.

Giff poured himself a drink and glancing up, caught the baffled and sullen expression in Welling's eyes. Giff passed the bottle to him and then downed his own drink feeling its slow warmth coil inside him. He felt someone beside him and glanced up to see Sheriff Edwards standing there. Fiske, seeing him too, put down his paper and said, "Have a drink with us, Sheriff."

Edwards reached out and took a cigar from the handful scattered in the middle of the table and said, "I'll have one of these instead." He sat down and, including them all in his question, asked without any real curiosity, "How did it go?"

Both Giff and Fiske waited for Welling to answer. He did finally, and in a discouraged voice. "It's a long haul, Sheriff. We'll get there, though."

Edwards lighted his cigar and asked, "Have you checked yet to see if anybody is collecting your reward?"

"I did. Nobody has," Giff said.

A faint flicker of malice came and vanished in Welling's eyes.

Edwards looked down at the tip of his cigar, then raised his glance to Welling, "What would the Land Office want with that particular issue of the *Free Press,* if it's any of my business?"

Fiske cleared his throat and said hurriedly, "Just a routine check of final proof notices for that issue. It was lost from the newspaper files."

Welling laughed shortly. "Don't you believe him, Sheriff," he said. His voice was already a little thick and blurred from the whiskey.

Giff cut in mildly, "If we get it, you'll know the whole story then, Sheriff."

"He could know it now if he wants," Welling said with a kind of alcoholic truculence as he regarded Giff.

Fiske folded his newspaper and rose; his casualness did not wholly cover the apprehension in his voice as he said, "Better come along before the barber shop's closed, Vince, or else we'll miss a hot bath."

But Welling had never taken his glance from Giff who was aware that Welling, with the unerring instinct of a heavy drinker in choosing the wrong moment, was about to pay off his grudge. Welling did not accept Fiske's invitation, and Giff thought bleakly, *Here it comes*.

Welling shuttled his glance to Edwards, "Are you a friend of Sebree's?" He did not give Edwards time to say one way or the other before he contined, "because if you are, you can tell him he's in trouble. He . . ."

Giff came to his feet then, saying thinly, "Shut up, Welling! You talk too much!"

Nothing could stop Welling and Giff saw it. For a brief second his impulse was to hit Welling and close his mouth. It was as if Welling read his thoughts, for he pushed his chair back out of Giff's reach and rose looking at Giff but talking to Edwards. "Once we get that issue of the *Free Press,* Sebree, Deyo and Kearie are on the way to jail."

Fiske sighed wearily, turned and left the table. Giff looked down at Edwards and saw the shock and the concern on the sheriff's face. He glanced up at Welling and saw the expression of fierce triumph in his eyes. In disgust and without any anger at all, he turned and tramped toward the door.

Welling's disclosure would be all over town in an hour, he knew. As long as people only read the reward notice and were in ignorance of the reason for the April seventeenth issue being wanted, there was a chance that one might be turned in to Welling. Now, with the threat of Sebree's punishment implicit, that faint chance was lessened. No man would hunt through a year's old newspapers on the off-chance that he could pick up fifty dollars it he knew that a bullet in the back went with it. Yet the harm was done and Welling had his brief moment of victory which, Giff supposed, was enough for him.

Halting on the plankwalk, Giff looked upstreet. Then the question that had been nagging at his mind for two days came unbidden again, and he was reminded once more of his conversation with Mrs. Sebree. Why had she said *Grady is afraid of Mary Kincheon?* Giff had wondered about that long enough; now he wanted to find out why she had said it.

He halted at the *Free Press* office and found it locked. Of a passing boy, he asked where Mary Kincheon lived and was told she had a room at the home of a widow named Mrs. Wiatt. He learned further that Mrs. Wiatt's house was a short distance down the side street from the second corner below.

Giff found the house easily and as he lifted the latch of the iron gate, he wondered who Wiatt had been, for this big brick house, nowhere near new, bespoke a one-time prosperity. The yard was full of flowers he could not identify and the big lawn was neatly trimmed. He caught the sweet smell of lilies of the valley as he mounted the steps and twisted the handle of the door bell.

The door was answered by a short, stout, gray-haired woman wearing a blue dress that just matched the color of her eyes. She did not greet him but stood as if barring his way until he presented his credentials.

Giff said, "Is Miss Kincheon home?"

"Does she know you?"

"Dixon is the name," Giff said. He saw a new interest mount in her eyes.

"Is this land office business?" Mrs. Wiatt asked.

Giff looked at her and could not keep a certain censure out of his voice as he said, "Would it make any difference if it wasn't?"

"It would," Mrs. Wiatt said promptly. "Mary is a pretty girl. If you're courting her, you've chosen the wrong time. Besides, you're dirty."

Giff said curtly, "Maybe she is too. We both work."

Giff took off his hat and followed her into the large

tidy parlor, confused and a little wary of this woman's strange behavior. She went on through the door, headed toward the back of the house and called, "Mary, a young man to see you." Then she came back into the parlor.

"How are you doing with those scoundrels at the Land Office?" she asked.

Giff could not hide the surprise he felt at her question. "That would be Mr. Deyo?" he asked.

Mrs. Wiatt nodded. "All of them. The ones that work in it and the ones that own it."

"Not very well," Giff said.

At that moment Mary stepped into the room. She was smoothing her dress with a telltale gesture of a woman who has just taken off her apron. She halted abruptly at the sight of Giff. "Not even a black eye. I'm surprised."

Giff shifted his feet uneasily and was aware that she was looking at the skinned knuckles of his hand that held his hat. He asked warily, "Should I have one?"

"Don't be modest," Mary said. "We've known about the fight at Torreon for two days."

Mrs. Wiatt asked promptly, "It wasn't Grady Sebree, was it?"

"No."

"Too bad," Mrs. Wiatt murmured. She looked at Mary now and there was a small devilment in her blue eyes. "Is it safe to leave you alone with him, Mary?"

"Heavens no," Mary said. "What is it you want, Mr. Dixon?"

Giff looked closely at her and wished for once she could be serious. He said, "It would only bore Mrs. Wiatt."

"Nonsense," Mrs. Wiatt said. "I'm never bored."

Giff said, "Not even by cooking supper?"

It was Mary who laughed then. Mrs. Wiatt good-naturedly accepted her defeat and said, "Don't be long, dears," as she left the room.

Giff nodded his head toward the door and said, "You two aren't related, are you?"

Mary smiled and shook her head in negation. "I

copy her. That's the only way I can bear working for Earl Kearie—by being a little crazy, I guess." She gestured toward a chair. "Sit down, please."

Giff sank into the closest chair, which was an uncomfortable one. He had no notion of how to begin this and only a very faint idea of what he wanted to say. However he framed it, the words would be too bald for this occasion. Mary had seated herself, and seeing his discomfort, made no move to ease it.

Giff plunged. "I met Mrs. Sebree at Torreon. Tell me something about her."

Mary studied him a moment, "Did you climb off a horse after a long day's ride to ask me that?"

"No, I'm just making talk," Giff admitted. "What about Mrs. Sebree?"

"She's a frightful hag," Mary said calmly. "But it isn't hard to understand why."

"Just what does it mean when a pretty woman calls an attractive woman a frightful hag?" Giff asked mildly. "Has she done something to you?"

"No," Mary said shortly. "I'm sorry I was uncharitable." She looked obliquely at him. "Do you think I'm pretty?"

Before Giff could answer, she said with total unconcern, "I withdraw that question. About Mrs. Sebree, now." She thought a moment. "I guess I hate her just because she's Mrs. Sebree. I hate anything connected with Sebree and that includes his wife."

"Any special reason for hating him?"

Mary shrugged. "Just on principle I guess. When you were little and read stories about the king in the castle and his happy, happy peasants, didn't you gag? Didn't you ever wonder if maybe just one peasant was unhappy at the king's having the power that he had? Didn't you think maybe just one of his subjects thought he had too much power? Couldn't one of the peasants hate the queen just because she was the king's wife?"

"Even queens can tell the truth sometimes. Does Mrs. Sebree happen to?"

Mary nodded emphatically. "So much so, it's embarrassing sometimes."

"Like it will be now," Giff murmured. A slow apprehension came into Mary's face as he continued, "Mrs. Sebree told me Grady is afraid of you."

Mary tried to laugh but the laugh didn't come off. Color mounted in her face and with quiet amazement Giff realized he had touched something private and important to her. He watched her, not helping her, seeing her mounting confusion. He judged that she was more frightened than angry; certainly for once she was inarticulate, and he waited.

"That's the most foolish thing she's ever said, and she's said a lot of them." Mary tried to make her tone light and failed. "Why would she want to say that?"

Giff didn't answer her and she shifted her position in the chair. "Really," she said earnestly, "you don't believe that do you?"

"Why do you care if I believe it or not?" Giff asked coldly. "Is it true?"

Now the anger came, or rather the illusion of anger and not its substance. "Why should I answer that question anyway?" she demanded vehemently. "What right have you to ask it?"

Giff didn't answer, only watched her.

The false anger vanished as quickly as it had appeared and in its place, as Mary leaned her elbows on her knees, was a sweet reasonableness. "Stop and think a moment," Mary said quietly. "I'm only a printer's devil. I help to run a broken down weekly newspaper and it just about pays for my food and clothes and shelter. Grady Sebree is a large stockholder and the manager of one of the biggest ranches in the Territory. Why should he fear me? You've just said I was pretty. Maybe it's Mrs. Sebree who fears my prettiness, although she has no cause to. I loathe Sebree and all he stands for; and I guess I loathe Mrs. Sebree most of all after this." Mary laughed suddenly and her laughter was genuine this time. "I'm beginning to loathe you."

The moment had gone; Mary had completely regained her composure. She said now, "Is it impertinent for me to ask how all this concerns your work for the land office?"

Giff rose saying, "I was wondering when you'd ask that question. It doesn't concern it at all."

Mary rose too, her smile once again warm and faintly mocking, "I am sure Mrs. Wiatt has counted on you for supper."

"Some other time," Giff said. "Will you thank her and tell her good-bye?"

Mary followed him to the door and on the porch he halted and put on his hat. He was about to bid her good evening when she said abruptly, "Why don't you come in some day and we'll talk about flowers or horses? I'm tired of snarling at you every time we meet."

"I'm tired of it too," Giff said. "Good night."

As he walked back the two blocks to the main street, the strangeness of this girl lingered in his mind. She was beautiful and had a needle-sharp and mocking cleverness, but she was hiding something. He had a disturbing conviction that Mrs. Sebree had told the truth, and he found himself disliking that truth. Minutes ago, Mary had asked him, *Did you climb off a horse after a long day's ride to ask me that?* That was exactly what he had done; he had hurried to her to find out if Mrs. Sebree was right. He could have waited to ask her, but he didn't, and now he wondered why. The answer came reluctantly. He had been in a terrible haste to hear her deny it. It was important to him that she should deny it, because he didn't want her to be mixed up with any man in this land swindle.

He wondered glumly, *Is she in it, too?* No, she had accepted his reward advertisement. If she were in it with Sebree, she would never have accepted it, because the finding of the paper would uncover her guilt. No, that wasn't it, yet Mrs. Sebree had spoken the truth, and he was none the wiser and considerably sadder for knowing it was the truth.

At the Family Cafe, he had a quick supper and then moved on to the livery, where he inquired the directions to Taltal of the hostler, and then helped himself to a fresh horse. There was still an hour of light left when the stage road began its climb to the distant peaks.

He was deep in the foothills when full darkness came and his thoughts turned again to Mary. He wondered what there had been in her life that had bred her dislike of Sebree. On principle she was entitled to dislike naked and arrogant power, but was that all that was behind her passion? Remembering her embarrassment at his questions, he knew there was something deeper and more personal than just principles. If it were something personal, why was she so careful to clothe it in those waspish generalities?

The stage road was lifting into thicker timber and the heavy scent of pine resin was in the air. He speculated idly on what he would learn in Taltal from Mrs. Bentham and why Mrs. Sebree had mentioned her. He had learned from the hostler that Taltal was a dreary, lonely stage stop at the bottom of a dark remote canyon. It was an odd place for a man to establish a mistress.

The up-stage passed him around nine o'clock; he rode in its persistent, hanging pennant of dust for another hour and when the last lingering smell of it was gone from the air, he saw the lamps of Taltal ahead through the thinly scattered spruce. The creek which he had forded many times below was now more narrow and its sound was a constant and pleasant part of the night.

As he crossed the bridge, he saw a half-dozen horses tied at the rail in front of the dimly lit building. He racked his horse among them, and dismounted. It was too dark to distinguish brands and he halted a moment considering this. If he struck a match and examined the horses, it would not go unnoticed by someone inside and would be a plain admission that he was wary of his company. He would have to take a chance that none of the horses was Torreon, for he knew that he was free game for Torreon hands in a place like this.

Mounting the steps, he entered the saloon. A game of poker was being played by four men at the far table.

They were strangers to him, and probably to each
other, he thought. Differing in features, they were basi-
cally alike, travel-weary, taciturn and suspicious. He
believed he knew their life well, for it had once been his
—a life of small and furtive dishonesties, of hunger,
of driving restlessness, of movement and solitude.

They regarded him covertly as he crossed the room
to the bar, and since his own dusty and unshaven
appearance matched theirs, they accepted him by ignoring him. He wondered if the bartender was Bentham. The man had the look of an old and cynical ex-
gambler who had lost his sharpness and his courage
with cards, Giff thought.

Bentham was washing glasses, and when he looked
up, Giff signaled for whiskey. Bentham, soiled towel
over his shoulder, took a glass and bottle from the
back bar, and set them silently on the bar before Giff.
The clicking of poker chips and the muted but sustained noise of the creek outside was interrupted occasionally by a word from the men behind him. He
had his drink, looking at the room and idly watching
the dexterity with which Bentham went about his job.
He wanted above all to establish the fact that he was in
no hurry, that he was an aimless drifter, a stranger.

He said presently, "Can a man get a room here and
bait for his horse?"

Bentham said, "For a dollar in advance, yes. No
breakfast."

Giff put two silver dollars on the bar top and got his
change back. Bentham said, "Which horse is yours?"
and when Giff told him the one farthest from the steps,
he left the room quietly. His air of tight-lipped and
studied silence was in keeping with this place, Giff
thought. He fashioned his cigarette, then strolled to
the door and looked out into the night. He saw a man,
not Bentham, come around the building, take his horse
and lead it around the far corner of the veranda. Giff's
brand, the livery brand, would probably go unnoticed
until the morning. There was a quality of somnolent
watchfulness about this place that began to push at

his nerves; he had a feeling that he had been tentatively sized up but that he would not be forgotten for a second until he rode out again.

Bentham returned to the room and Giff wheeled and tramped over to him as he stood in the doorway. "Room number five," Bentham said, "at your right, upstairs."

"Is it too late for me to get something to eat?" Giff asked. He was not hungry, but he wanted to stir up movement in the place on the off chance that he would see Mrs. Bentham.

Bentham said, "I'll see," and crossed the dining room to the kitchen door. In a moment he appeared and said as he passed toward the barroom, "Go on in the kitchen."

Giff went through the kitchen door and halted by the stove. A dark-haired girl with her back to him was cutting bread at the sink counter. Giff said, "Is there some place I can wash out back?"

The girl turned and Giff knew at once that this was Sebree's Mrs. Bentham. She had a sullen sort of beauty that was not attractive to him, but was undeniable. Her dress was bright and clean and Giff thought, *Sebree would teach her that.*

"There's a pump out back." Her voice held an undertone of resentment of having to serve him at this hour.

He went on through the kitchen and washed up at the pump. When he returned, a place was set at the oilcloth-topped kitchen table and a cup of coffee was already poured. He sat down and sipped at his coffee, watching the quick deft movements of Mrs. Bentham as she prepared her food, wondering how to approach her.

Take a chance, he thought and now he spoke pleasantly, "Mrs. Sebree sends her regards to you."

If he had hoped to startle her by these words, he succeeded almost too well. She dropped a knife that clanged on the counter and rattled into the sink. In the same movement she wheeled to face him, an expression of both amazement and fear in her face. Slowly, she got control of herself and then took three slow steps to the far side of the table. "Who are you?" she demanded suspiciously.

"Don't worry; Grady didn't send me." Giff replied. Then he asked in a mild voice, "Is my supper ready?"

"Did Mrs. Sebree send you up here?"

Giff shook his head in negation, "No, she just said to say hello to you."

For a full ten seconds Mrs. Bentham regarded him with an alert wariness. She said then, "She doesn't even know me."

"She knows *of* you," Giff said. He could see that she was weighing in her mind the significance of his words. She was puzzled, expecting trouble, wondering how to prepare for it. He repeated, "Is my supper ready?"

She turned reluctantly to her work and then crossed to him with a plate of cold steaks and cold fried potatoes.

He put his attention to the food, ignoring the girl; she had returned to the counter and put her back against it and was watching him. Giff had an idea that she would not let this rest here, but he ate unconcernedly. After a few moments he asked around a mouthful of food, "Stage crowded tonight?"

Mrs. Bentham started in surprise at the sound of his voice. He could see she was plainly surprised at the irrelevance of his words, and impatient too. She said, "Just who *are* you?"

He heard footsteps in the dining room at the same moment Mrs. Bentham did and now he watched her carefully, hoping for a hint as to what course to follow. She lifted her head in sudden alarm and then moved quickly toward the stove. She picked up the coffee-pot and as the door opened and Bentham came in, she walked to the table and freshened Giff's cup of coffee. Afterward she moved to the cupboard above the sink, opened it and reached up for a can. When she had set it on the counter, she opened a drawer and took out a can opener. *She's afraid of him,* Giff thought.

He looked up indifferently at Bentham who was standing in the kitchen door, then looked down at his plate and continued eating. Presently Bentham backed into the dining room and the door swung shut. He saw Mrs. Bentham pause in her movements, cock her head and listen. Then she glanced at him and raised her finger to her lips. Giff nodded and continued eating in silence. After a few moments, he heard a board creak in the dining room and he knew that Bentham, satisfied with his eavesdropping, had returned to the bar.

When Bentham returned to the saloon, he saw Perez, his hired man, standing beside the outer door, hat in hand, waiting for him.

He crossed to the Mexican and asked softly, *"Quién es?"*

The Mexican lifted his shoulders in a shrug, and then said in Spanish, "I don't know him. His horse carries the livery stable brand."

"Murray's?"

Perez nodded, and Bentham said, "All right. Good night."

When Perez had left the porch, Bentham stepped out into the night and walked slowly to the porch rail. The presence of one of Cass Murray's horses here was suspicious in itself. An out-at-the-pants drifter couldn't afford to ride one, and if he'd come from town why was he staying here tonight?

Memory of Murray's name still lingered, teasing at him. What had he heard about Murray lately from the stage driver? Oh yes, that Murray had first hired this drifter that was making so much—

He turned, suddenly, realization coming abruptly. This man was Dixon, the land office chainman who had broken Traff's jaw and had cleaned out the Torreon bunkhouse. Yes, his looks jibed with the stage driver's description of him—"a tall, black-Irishman with a go-to-hell look in his eyes."

Bentham speculated closely for a moment on what Dixon was doing here. *He's after Sebree—maybe through his woman,* Bentham thought.

He hoped bitterly that Dixon would succeed.

For two long years Bentham had bided his time,

taking Sebree's orders, and fronting for his woman. And not one of these days had passed without his hoping and watching for some way to even the score with Sebree. He had thought of several ways; but after examining them he backed away from them, for they took something he had precious little of, and that was courage. He had the courage to face down a saloon drunk; that was a trick and took only steady nerves. But Sebree was different. He knew that the longer he waited the more servile he was becoming—and the more his hatred of Sebree grew.

Now, thinking of Dixon, he began to wonder. Casting back to everything he had heard about the man, his wonder grew into speculation. Dixon, he had already guessed, was the reason for Sebree's wanting Jim Archer. The very fact that Sebree was that afraid of Dixon pushed Bentham to his decision now, and the thought *Maybe he can do it*. He stepped down into the night and circled the hotel. Approaching the back door, he walked slowly and quietly until he could touch it. The sound of Dixon's and his wife's voices inside was a low, indistinguishable murmur.

Bentham calculated, then. Both of them inside would be listening for sounds in the dining room. Knowing that, he put his hand on the doorknob and slowly turned it. When the latch opened silently, he pushed the door open until a tiny crack of light showed. Simultaneously, he picked up the sound of his wife's bitter voice in mid-speech. "—all this way to tell me about Mrs. Sebree. What is it you want from me?"

"Your help."

"In what? Sending Grady to jail?"

Dixon's voice was dry. "Odd you should say that. I didn't mention jail. Has he done anything that would put him there?"

Bentham heard his wife's voice turn sullen as she answered. "I don't know. I hear talk, though."

I bet you do, Bentham thought grimly.

"About what?" Dixon asked her.

"Oh, I don't know, I tell you!"

"You know he's in trouble now," Dixon prodded.

His wife was quiet a moment; Bentham wondered if she would answer. "Yes, I overhear talk from stage passengers and the drivers."

"But what's he said about it to you? Think back. If he hasn't told you about it, then he thinks you don't know about it. He'd naturally be careless. Has he said or done anything you don't understand?"

Dixon's voice was persuasive, and Bentham knew he was softening Sarita.

"Yes, I overheard—" Sarita's voice ceased, and Bentham's pulse quickened. What had she overheard?

"You overheard what?"

"Nothing." Sarita's voice was flat, scared.

"You're afraid of him, aren't you?" Dixon jibed.

"You don't know Grady," Sarita said dully. "He'd have it out of me if he suspected I'd even seen you."

She's whipped, Bentham thought. He'd heard enough to know Dixon could talk until midnight and get nothing more out of her. Softly, he closed the door, and then moved off into the night.

Pausing, he felt an odd excitement within him. Dixon was the kind of reckless tenacious fool who wouldn't be stopped. His very presence here testified to that. *Then why not help him?* Bentham asked himself. They were both after the same thing.

Then, thinking of Sarita and her fear of Grady, Bentham knew he must play this carefully. She mustn't suspect anything. After a moment's thought, he moved around the corner of the saloon and went inside. The poker game was still in progress, and none of the players noticed him as he went behind the bar, lifted out a gun from under it, and tucked it in the waistband of his pants, then went out into the dining room.

Giff had heard the footsteps in the dining room, and he ceased talking. The door swung open silently; and after putting down his cup of coffee, Giff glanced up.

Bentham was standing in the doorway, a gun in his hand held hip high. His chill, malignant eyes regarded Giff closely.

"I got a look at the brand on your horse," Bentham said. "It's a livery horse of Murray's."

Giff waited, watching.

"You aren't riding through."

"I don't recall saying I was."

Bentham watched him a bitter moment. "You're Dixon aren't you?"

Giff only nodded and gathered his legs under him to move. Only the belief that Bentham had not reached the point of decision held him longer in his chair.

"Go saddle your horse and clear out of here," Bentham said thinly. "Sarita, light a lantern."

Mrs. Bentham moved around behind Giff and he could hear her take down the lantern, fumble nervously at the wall-box of matches and strike a light. Bentham never ceased watching him and now the old man said, "Take it."

Giff turned in his chair and accepted the lighted lantern from Mrs. Bentham. She hurriedly passed him and went out of the room hugging the wall and careful to keep out of the way of her husband's leveled gun.

"Do I go now?"

"Get up." Bentham moved in behind Giff as he turned toward the back door. Outside, Bentham directed him to the corral. For a dismal moment, Giff wondered if this was only Bentham's way of moving him outside where there would be no witnesses to the kill. The flesh on his back crawled; he kept remembering the dead cold eyes of the man holding the gun. A break into the night would only bring it quicker, he knew; and he tramped on.

When he reached the corral, he saw his horse nuzzling the last of the hay that had been forked from the shed. With the corral poles between them, he might have a chance, he thought; he hung the lantern on the gatepost and reached for the wire latch.

Suddenly Bentham's voice from behind him said quietly, "She'll be watching from the house. Keep on working while I talk. Do you understand that?"

Giff didn't, but he said yes as he opened the gate. He walked over to his saddle atop the corral and Bentham spoke in a low voice, "Sebree came to me the other night and asked me if I could send out for a reliable killer. I sent for him and he'll be paid five hundred dollars for killing a man."

Giff lifting the bridle from the top pole of the corral, moved over to his horse. "Who is it to be?" he asked without turning.

"You."

Giff slipped the bit into his dun's mouth and then moved back for his saddle. He glanced obliquely at Bentham, hoping the man's expression would give some clue to the cause of his treason. Bentham's news carried little surprise for him, but its manner of telling did. There was no time to follow it through now for Bentham was talking again. "The man's name will be Jim Archer. His instructions are to put up at the Territory House and wait until Sebree gets in touch with him. Have you got that?"

"I have, but have you?" As Giff heaved the saddle off the corral top, he glanced again at Bentham. There was a puzzlement in the man's face. Giff asked, tramping toward his horse, "Are you ready to leave here?"

"If I have to."

"You have to, and the sooner the better." He slacked the saddle to the ground and put the saddle blanket on his horse.

Bentham's voice was directed at his back, "I don't get it."

Giff heaved the saddle up on his horse's back, then pulled the horse around so that he could look across the saddle at Bentham. "I'll get this Archer," Giff said quietly. "When I do, Sebree will know who pointed him out to me." He saw Bentham considering this with a wry carefulness.

Giff gathered up his reins, stepped into the saddle, and pulled his horse toward the gate. Bentham, stepping aside, said, "It's time anyway—past time." He looked up as Giff passed him and said in a low voice, "Don't thank me. Just get Sebree."

And then Giff passed him, heading for the canyon road.

5

It was Sheriff Edwards' custom to open the store each morning, wait the few minutes until the first clerk arrived and then walk the two blocks to the county courthouse and assign his deputies their day's work. This morning, however, he unlocked the door and, instead of spending a pleasant interval watching the town come to work, he tramped down the main aisle toward the back stairs.

His conversation with Welling last evening had brought him a sleepless night and sober hours of self-searching; sometime during the small hours of the morning, he had come to the conclusion he was acting upon now. It was plain to him that Sebree was in deep trouble, and that the April seventeenth issue of the *Free Press* lying in the store's basement files would turn that trouble into catastrophe.

But it was trouble with the *federal* government, not the county, Edwards reasoned. County officers were not bound to aid the federal government unless ordered— and nobody had ordered him. On the other hand, Sebree had been generous to him. Besides being the store's best customer, Sebree was the real power in the county. He had ordered Edwards' election; and then had asked few favors, all of them reasonable, in return. Because that left Edwards his self-respect, he felt in some obscure way that he was honor bound to help Sebree. The least he could do in return then was to destroy the evidence which would convict Sebree of a federal offense. He would leave judgment of the ethics of Sebree's crimes to others who knew the facts, he told himself.

He struck several matches on his way down the dark passage to the newspaper files, and when finally, his hand shaking nervously, he contrived to light the lamp, he paused a moment and reminded himself that there was no special hurry. Yet there was, he knew. If Arthur Miles saw him coming up from the basement at this hour of the morning, he might suspect his errand; and Edwards did not want to share his secret with anyone.

Kneeling before the stack of *Free Press*es, he thumbed through them until he came to the April twenty-fourth issue. Below it was the April tenth issue and for a baffled moment Edwards read and reread the dates. When if finally came to him after further search that the April seventeenth issue was missing, he rose slowly, fighting down the panic rising within him.

Only Arthur Miles could have taken it, he knew, for Arthur was the only employee who knew the filing system existed. The longer he pondered this the more certain he was that it could only have been Arthur. His reason for taking it would be innocent enough. The whole town, as well as Edwards, knew that gambling was Arthur's weakness; Henty's monte table had cost him the store and it devoured a good half of his monthly earnings. He wanted that copy of the *Free Press* for the real pleasure he would have in gambling away the fifty dollars Welling would pay for it.

Edwards slowly moved over to the lamp and blew it out. It would not be difficult to retrieve the newspaper from Arthur. No man was fool enough to lose his job over fifty dollars, and Edwards intended to use that threat.

Making his way to the stairs, Edwards hastened up them. A glance at the first floor assured him that all the clerks were on hand. He climbed the balcony steps and halted at the head of them. Arthur had not arrived yet. Edwards glanced at his watch, saw that it was some minutes after seven-thirty and crossed to his desk. He opened the safe, brought out his business papers and got down to work. But it was impossible for him to concentrate on anything until Arthur arrived.

By eight o'clock he had given up trying to work and watched the doorway for Arthur's entrance. By eight-thirty he was certain something was wrong; either Arthur was ill or, what was more likely, he was afraid to come to work for fear Edwards had discovered his theft.

Edwards rose then, put on his hat and went down stairs. On his way out, he paused long enough to ask of one of the clerks if Arthur had come to work that morning. Nobody, the clerk said, had seen him.

On the plankwalk, a thought came to Edwards that appalled him. What if Arthur had already taken the newspaper to Welling? Could he be with him now, this very moment? It would explain Arthur's absence from the store. He must find out.

Almost at a run, Edwards crossed the street and entered the hotel lobby. Pausing at the dining room door, he glanced in and saw Welling eating a solitary breakfast at one of the window tables. Edwards breathed a shaky sigh of relief, removed his hat and crossed the room, nodding occasionally to the diners he recognized.

Welling, at his approach, said affably, "Good morning, Sheriff. Have a cup of coffee with me?"

Edwards declined with thanks and asked, "Has your copy of the *Free Press* turned up?"

A kind of embarrassed uneasiness touched Welling and he shook his head in negation. "It's hardly had time."

"I suppose you're right," Edwards said. He excused himself abruptly and left the room. He was safe so far, but he must find Arthur promptly. He would hunt the town, beginning at Arthur's house.

Miles's home, a block past the ugly yellow brick courthouse, was set in a large uncared-for lot, bordered by tall cottonwoods; and it had once been one of the town's substantial homes. Now its paint was peeling and the plantings around the house were running wild. The gate in the picket fence had been left open for so long onto the cinder sidewalk that a path was worn in the weeds around it. Edwards mounted the rickety

steps, knocked on the door and received no answer.
Maybe he's ill, he thought suddenly; it he were, he
could not be expected to answer the door, so Edwards
knocked again and stepped inside.

He had his mouth open to call when his voice died
in his throat. The dusty close room was in a monumental disorder, with books, papers, clothes and dishes
littering its chairs and its worn floor. Obviously the
room had been ransacked.

A kind of dread touched Edwards as he beheld it.
In the far wall a door opened into a room beyond
and Edwards crossed the room to it, and on the sill
halted abruptly.

On the faded bedroom carpet lay Arthur's body,
the stain of blood long since shed darkening the carpet
beneath him.

The ransacked house and the lifeless body before
him told Edwards all he needed to know. The newspaper would be gone and Arthur had probably died
defending it.

From whom? Edwards already had the answer to
that question. The government allowed no employee
to murder in its name, so it couldn't have been Welling.
That leaves Sebree, Edwards thought calmly. The cor-
ollary of that thought was like a cold hand of fear that
touched Edwards' shoulder. *It's up to me to arrest him.*

Edwards hesitated only a moment while he made
his bitter choice. Then he set about righting the disor-
dered room, in a hurry to begin covering up.

Corazon's early risers were the teamsters who had
horses to curry and harness before their day's work
could begin. This morning Giff had breakfast among
them at the Family Cafe, and afterward, when he
stepped out into Grant Street, it was deserted save for
a pair of romping dogs, whose capers stirred up thin
streams of soft dust.

He turned at the land office corner, his half boots
ringing hollowly on the deserted plankwalk. Three
blocks beyond he saw Cass at his town-farming. This
was the hour, he knew, that Cass preferred to be alone

with his garden; and when Giff reached the half-block plot, he hunkered down on his heels against the trunk of a bordering cottonwood and had his after breakfast cigarette.

Cass saw him, but continued hoeing his corn for another few minutes. Then, finishing the row, he shouldered his hoe and tramped over to where Giff was sitting. There was a kind of tranquillity in Cass's round face that Giff envied; and neither man spoke immediately.

Cass sat down beside him and had his look at his crop, which, in its strange setting amongst the tall trees and houses of the town, was nevertheless a balanced farm in miniature.

Presently, Giff said, "Cass, a new man will come to town in three or four days. He'll put up at the Territory House. His name will be Jim Archer." Now he looked at Cass. "Suppose you could let me know when he comes in?"

"Where'll you be?"

"That's just it, I don't know. But you can always find me."

"Who is he?" Cass asked. "Land Office?"

Giff smiled faintly at the thought, but only shook his head. "Just a man I want to see when he gets here."

"Sure," Cass said, and his curiosity ended there. He plucked a stem of grass and chewed thoughtfully on it for a silent interval. Then he said, "Your boss spilled over at the mouth again, didn't he?"

Giff nodded. "So that's around town by now?"

"Is it true that the paper you advertised for will put Sebree, Deyo and Kearie in jail?"

Giff said it was.

Cass thought about that a moment. "You'll never get it now, you know. Sebree will have a man watching in the hotel lobby. A man would be signing his death warrant to ask for Welling."

"I know," Giff said glumly.

Cass removed the straw from his mouth and looked

at it, speculatively, "How did you ever get that reward notice in the *Free Press* to begin with?"

"Mary Kincheon."

Cass looked sidelong at him, "Think you could do it again?"

Giff didn't know. Mary had never mentioned any trouble between Kearie and herself over the placing of the notice; and thinking of it now, he considered it strange that she hadn't. Had Kearie, once the harm was done, accepted it philosophically as an employee's mistake and never mentioned the matter to her? Giff did not, however, know what Cass was driving at and he said, "Suppose I could?".

"Well, if a man had a copy of that paper you wanted, he could write and tell you so, and you could come and get it. Sebree would never know he'd written."

Giff considered this a brief moment, liking it. If the invitation to write Welling were published, it would cancel the implicit threat to anyone helping him, he knew. He said, "It might work, Cass. We'll try it."

They talked then about other things as the town came to life around them. A barefoot boy drove a cow, her heavy udders swinging, past them to the morning milking. An occasional merchant or clerk, enjoying the cool of this morning hour and the sight of Cass's planting, passed them, giving Cass good morning.

Presently Giff rose and Cass hauled himself to his feet and together they walked back to the livery. Giff parted with him there and headed for the *Free Press* office.

He found himself liking the prospect of seeing Mary again; and he wondered, in view of what had passed between them yesterday, if she would be the same. The front office of the *Free Press* was empty, and from the rear came the same soft chunking of metal upon metal that he had heard on his first visit. Walking back, he halted by the type stand.

Mary, seated on the stool, had heard him enter and was waiting to identify her visitor. He saw the small start of pleasure in her eyes as she recognized him.

"What'll it be, flowers or horses?" she asked, putting down the stick of type in her hand.

Giff remembered their parting yesterday and he touched his hat and gave her a spare smile. "Can we put that off?"

"So, it's business again."

Giff didn't answer. He looked around the shop and said, "I thought Kearie promised you a new printer."

"He's on order. But you know printers—they are a little brighter than your boss, but they are just as thirsty. I ought to know; my father was one." She wiped her ink-stained hands on the front of her heavy apron and then came around the stand and walked to her desk saying, "This new one is probably drinking up his pay in a Vegas saloon. He'll be along."

This was the first clue Giff had to her past and as he followed her across the office, he asked curiously, "Did your father run a newspaper?"

Mary sat down, and she grimaced wryly, "Yes, he ran them and from them. From Indiana to California and back here. I learned to set type because I had to if we were to eat. Sometimes we didn't."

"He owned the *Free Press?*"

Mary nodded. "Years ago. He took it over for five months' back pay. And it was his big chance." She shrugged. "He missed it."

"Booze?" Giff asked.

Mary nodded. "It was that finally, but not to begin with. When he first took it over, it meant a great deal to him. He'd been printing other men's opinions for so long that he almost forgot he had any himself. When he first took over, he remembered those opinions and spoke up—for a while."

"What changed his mind?"

Mary looked searchingly at him. "Grady Sebree."

Giff's interest quickened. Perhaps she would tell him now the real reason for hating Sebree. He said nothing, waiting for her to go on.

"Oh, it's not what you think," she said quietly. "Grady never threatened him or even told him he didn't like what Dad printed. He shut him up another way."

Giff watched her in puzzlement.

"Dad started out by sticking up for the homesteader, and the little rancher. Sebree never whined when Dad hit him in print. As a matter-of-fact, he would come in and talk it over. He flattered Dad by asking his advice."

"On what things?"

Mary shrugged. "Oh, nothing important. Did Dad think it was time to ship, or should Torreon wait? Who did Dad think would make a good Sheriff? Did Dad like the government policy toward the Indians? It was just anything—but Dad was flattered."

She paused and Giff waited, and presently Mary went on, her voice bitter. "Pretty soon, Dad got to talking like Sebree. He copied his opinions after Sebree. He forgot the ordinary man, and started beating a drum for the big cattle interests. He wasn't his own man any more. Sebree's flattery and friendship had corrupted him. He borrowed money from Sebree, who was glad to lend it to him. No bribes were ever paid and no threats were made, but he wound up a fawning tool of Sebree's." She looked at him. "Do you see how that could happen to a weak man?"

Giff nodded.

"He began to drink in earnest, once he realized he'd been neutralized and put on Sebree's shelf. It killed him, finally. I sold the paper to Kearie to pay off the money Dad had borrowed."

"And then stayed on to work for him?"

Mary shrugged. "It was the easiest thing to do." She gave a short laugh. "The easiest thing to do," she repeated. "I guess I am my father's daughter!" She looked up at him almost soberly as if this talk were not pleasant, "Is this instead of horses or flowers?"

Giff put a leg up on the desk, looked down at her and nodded. "It's a subject I like better."

Mary looked pleased. "Then trade with me," she said. "All I know about you is that Dr. Miller pried a pound of buckshot out of your front."

Giff scowled, although he was not aware of it, and a look of uneasiness came into his dark face. "Well, I can't ever remember not being around cattle. I grew up North-South, from Texas to Montana. It doesn't matter where, because they were all alike."

Mary said, "I'll bet you were in school more than I was."

"I learned the alphabet from directions on a baking powder can," Giff challenged.

"There are worse teachers," Mary said. "For one, a sheriff's summons."

They both smiled at this and were both silent a moment, as if this sharing of their hard childhood years opened a new and friendly intimacy between them.

Mary asked suddenly, "Where do you go when this is finished?"

"I haven't thought," Giff answered slowly, almost reluctantly.

"Don't you want something of your own, something besides a horse?"

Giff nodded, "I have for a long time, but you don't start a herd on trail driver's wages. You can get awfully hungry just watching calves grow up." He realized then that his voice had dropped to a sour roughness; he could see the dislike of it in Mary's eyes and he knew this moment of confession was ended. He was just as glad; he had never meant to get into it anyway.

Sliding off the desk, he reached in his shirt pocket for his sack of tobacco, wondering how to frame his request for another advertisement. He took a long time to fashion his cigarette and before it was finished the door opened and Earl Kearie stepped in. When Giff turned and saw him standing there, his black suit smeared with the chalk dust of a thousand billiard games, his bony, sallow face holding an iron-hard dislike, he knew he had waited too long. *She wouldn't have taken it anyway,* he told himself. but the thought of Kearie's ill-timed entrance rankled.

From beside the door, Kearie demanded, "What are you doing here?"

"Always the businessman," Mary cut in sardonically to Kearie. "Give him a chance to tell me."

"I saw him come in ten minutes ago. He hasn't any

business with you," Kearie said flatly. "If this is social, you can save it till later. If it isn't, then the answer is no more reward notices printed. Tell him to get out."

Giff said softly, "Tell me yourself."

Kearie came over closer to the desk and halted. "You won't get away with it again, Dixon." His voice was flat and angry. "We accept nothing from Welling to be printed in this paper. You were lucky to get by with it once. If I'd been here, you wouldn't have."

"Try being here sometime," Mary taunted.

Giff asked dryly, "Are you having her watched now?"

"That's right."

Giff glanced at Mary and then back at Kearie. "Is she obeying your orders?"

A slow smile lifted Kearie's upper lip. Watching Giff, he said, "Mary, I want you to run this notice tomorrow. Have you got a pencil?"

"Is that the notice?" Mary jibed.

Kearie continued as if he had not heard, "This is the notice: Five hundred dollars reward will be paid for the delivery of each and every complete copy of the April seventeenth, 1882, issue of the *San Dimas County Free Press* to the undersigned. Grady Sebree, Torreon Ranch, Corazon, Territory of New Mexico."

Giff felt a sudden discouragement then. If this offer were printed, it, coupled with Welling's disclosure of yesterday, would end all hope of them getting the April seventeenth copy. Five hundred dollars was a sum the land office could not match in its reward offer. Both fear of Sebree and the amount of money he was offering would insure Torreon's getting any issue of that date that existed. It was a clever move and one that cut the ground from under Welling.

When he looked at Mary, there was a lingering surprise still in her face. He asked, "Are you going to print that?" He did not understand the lingering look Mary gave Kearie then. It held something secret and challenging, as if Kearie's words carried more and different meaning to her than it had to him. Finally she glanced up at him and said tonelessly, "He has to say on that."

She would have to print it, Giff knew, and for a
moment, watching the open malice in Kearie's face, he
tasted the bitter flavor of defeat. An offer of five hundred dollars would send every housewife in this corner of the Territory scurrying to the attic to see if she
had saved the copy. Prodded by the size of the reward,
someone was sure to turn it up—to be delivered into
Sebree's hands.

Kearie said then, smugness in his tone, "There's
such a thing as being so sharp you cut your own throat.
Sebree would never have thought of the reward except
for your reward notice."

Giff didn't answer; he was wondering how to pre-
vent Sebree's reward offer from being published. A few
days' grace might mean all the difference in the world
to the success of Welling's investigation. Sebree's news
would kill it.

Suddenly, he found himself remembering his first
meeting with Mary and her derisive description of
Kearie and his neglect of his newspaper. *He can't set
type,* Giff thought, *and there's no printer. It has to be
Mary.*

He looked searchingly at Mary, wondering. No, he
couldn't ask her to refuse. She had a living to earn. *But
what if I make it impossible for her to set it.* He glanced
idly back into the shop, and his glance settled on the
type stand.

Then he rammed his hands in his hip pockets, stared
at the floor and began to slowly pace the room.

Kearie chuckled. "Thanks for the idea."

On his slow circle, Giff looked up at him, then away.
When his circle reached the rear of the type stand, he
acted swiftly. With a savage lunge, he hurled his shoulder against the type stand. The upper case tray tilted
over, and then the whole stand rose on its front legs,
teetered and crashed into the composing table where
the forms were laid out. The falling case took the
composing table with it too; there was a mighty crash,
and then the thousands of pieces of type from the
case and from the forms cascaded onto the floor in
one discordant metallic jangle.

He wheeled and saw Kearie, his mouth open, rooted in his tracks. Mary had come to her feet, a look of consternation on her face.

"Can you sort out type, Kearie?" Giff asked quietly.

Kearie found his voice then. "Why you damned idiot! We have a paper to get out! We . . ." Kearie understood it then; his wrath was controlled as he said, "All you've done is make a night's work for Mary."

Giff watched Mary as she moved past him and halted beside the shattered case, her stance uneven from the scattered type underfoot. Then she looked up at him and he saw that she too understood the reason for his act. Kearie could not sort out this tangle in a week. Unless Mary labored at it, there would be no paper for days. The choice was squarely up to her. For long seconds she seemed to be considering this and then she regarded Kearie. "Say that again," she said coldly.

"I said it only meant a night's work for you," Kearie repeated and there was undisguised threat in his voice. Mary began to laugh then. It started softly and grew into a wild, almost uncontrolled laughter. She moved past Giff to the desk and sat down. Giff listened for a note of hysteria in her laughter and found none; it was a laugh of pure hilarity and he was reassured.

Kearie looked at her as if she had gone mad. He came over to the desk finally and put both bony hands on it and said, "Stop it! Stop it! You hear?"

Mary's laughter slowly ceased, and when she could talk she said to Kearie, "Even if you knew the alphabet, it would be funny, Earl. But the letters will be upside down to you. Even the final proof notices set up in the forms are pied. And they're six-point, so small you'd need a magnifying glass to read them—if you could read." She began to laugh again, and this time Giff smiled. The deep flush in Kearie's sallow face was a measure of his bafflement and rage. Mary stopped laughing again long enough to say, "It would take me three or four days to sort it out. It'll take you a month. Happy hunting."

Kearie said harshly, "Stop that now! You've got to get to work. Tomorrow's press day."

Mary leaned back in her chair and only shook her head slowly from side to side. "It *was* press day, you mean. Lord knows when the next one is."

"You won't do it?" Kearie asked unbelievingly.

"No," Mary said flatly. "Not even if you give me the newspaper."

This was what Giff had been waiting to hear. He moved quietly across the room, put a hand on the door and raised his other hand to his hat brim in salute to Mary before he stepped out.

Kearie had been watching Mary so intently that he did not notice Giff's departure. He heard the door close, swiveled his head, saw Giff had gone, then returned his attention to Mary. "You can't quit!"

Mary said coldly, "Is Sebree in town?"

Kearie stared at her blankly. "What? I don't know— oh yes, he is. What's that got to do with what I'm talking about?"

Mary said, "Have him at Deyo's office in half an hour. You'd better be there too."

Slow suspicion mounted in Kearie's face. He was torn between the wild need to persuade Mary to stay and between dread at this new and undefined threat of Mary's.

"Look," he began persuasively, "let's settle this now. You've got . . ."

"Go away," Mary said coldly. "You be at Deyo's."

At ten o'clock Mary mounted the steps of the land office and went in. A few feet beyond the door her way was barred by a long counter. Plat books were stacked helter-skelter on its surface; an elderly Mexican clerk wearing alpaca sleeve guards had left his desk under the big front window to confer with a man at the counter. Beyond the racks of files and in the back wall were two doors. One was closed and on its opaque glass was painted RECEIVER; the other was open and Mary saw Ross Deyo sitting at his desk. He was talking earnestly to someone Mary could not see except for his boots, and Mary identified those as belonging to Sebree.

She was a familiar in this office and she lifted the counter gate, stepped inside and closed it, then crossed the big room and stepped into the register's office. It was a large room holding, besides the roll-top desk, four barrel chairs lined against the wall. Sebree and Earl Kearie occupied two of them. They rose along with Deyo at her entrance and Mary, nodding indifferently, closed the door behind her.

A pleasant feeling of malice came to Mary as she accepted the chair Sebree offered her and sat down. Deyo's jowly face held an uneasy apprehension; Kearie looked worried and beaten. Only Sebree, as he sat down and drew a pale cigar from his shirt pocket and lighted it, seemed at ease.

He puffed his cigar until it was burning evenly; then regarded Mary with a fatherly expression that Mary knew was wholly false. "I hope you aren't serious about leaving Kearie," Sebree said mildly. "He's in a hole."

"One hundred feet deep," Mary agreed.

"It's too late to get a printer up from Vegas in time for tomorrow," Sebree went on reasonably. "Why don't you stay on until he comes? If Kearie misses this issue, you know, he'll be in trouble with the government, since he's contracted to publish all these legal forms on specified dates."

"Can't he talk?" Mary asked dryly nodding toward Kearie.

Sebree looked at Kearie, "Of course."

"Well, I don't want to hear him then," Mary said. "You either. I didn't call you here to listen to you bargain with me about working." She paused. "It's about the other."

There was a short silence, during which Kearie and Deyo exchanged brief and worried glances. Sebree, however, merely raised an eybrow and continued to regard her.

"What about it?" Sebree asked.

"The price has gone up," Mary said quietly.

There was another silence. Both Kearie and Deyo looked helplessly at Sebree.

"What put that in your mind?" Sebree asked.

"You're offering five hundred dollars for each copy of the April seventeenth issue, aren't you?"

Sebree nodded.

"That makes my copy—or Albers' copy if you like— at least five hundred dollars more valuable," Mary said.

Sebree stroked one side of his mustache with the third finger of the hand which was holding his cigar. His mild gaze was almost reflective and certainly unworried. "There's a difference in the two, my dear," he said then. "If I offer five hundred dollars for that issue, I pay when it's delivered into my hands. You won't deliver your copy. You'll simply threaten to turn it over to the government unless I keep paying. There's a difference, you see."

"I do see," Mary said sweetly. "But it's too fine a difference to bother with." She paused to isolate this, "The price has gone up to one thousand dollars."

"Which I will pay on delivery of your copy," Sebree answered.

Mary sighed and stood up, "Well don't ever say I didn't give you a chance."

A faint thrust of alarm came into Sebree's mild eyes but he chuckled softly. "That's no way to bargain, Mary."

Mary looked down at him and said coldly, "That's what you don't understand, Grady—I'm not bargaining. I simply want another thousand dollars from you three. In return I promise not to deliver the paper to Welling."

"But you retain the paper," Sebree said stubbornly. He leaned forward in his chair now and said earnestly, "You make a poor crook, Mary. The very essence of blackmail is not to crowd it too far. You're crowding it."

Mary nodded in agreement. "I have to."

Sebree's eyebrows lifted. "Why? Has something happened?"

"Not yet, but it will," Mary said. "You of all people should see that."

Sebree frowned and his gaze still held hers. "Explain that to me."

"Giff Dixon," Mary said slowly. "He's going to pull down the roof on all of us."

"And whose fault will it be if he does?" Sebree asked coldly. *"You* were the one who accepted his reward notice for the April seventeenth copy. *You* printed it without showing it to Kearie or me or Deyo. That started him out."

"Are you scolding me again?" Mary asked calmly. "I explained that. I printed it because I knew it would scare you. I knew it would double the value of my copy or make it worthless. It's doubled it. That's what I'm telling you now, thanks to Dixon."

"But now you're scared of him," Sebree pointed out. "He's stampeding you."

His tone was mildly scoffing and, hearing it, Mary felt a sudden and unexplained anger. She spoke with a corrosive scorn then. "What kind of a judge of men are you, Sebree? He knows you killed Albers; he told the whole town. He laid that bully boy-foreman of yours flat on a saloon floor with a broken jaw. He went right into your cookshack and beat up one of your hands. He put Kearie out of business just as surely as if he had taken a sledge hammer to the press. And you aren't worried!"

Sebree's faint smile lifted a corner of his mustache. "He'll be taken care of at the right time."

A cold alarm touched Mary then and held her mute for a moment. "Oh no he won't! Not by you!" Her voice had a faint quaver in it that she could not suppress, as she went on, "That's why I keep the paper. If anything happens to Dixon, Welling gets my copy. You could get away with his murder as far as Edwards is concerned, but try it and the big, bad federal government has caught up with you."

"Sit down, please," Sebree said wearily.

Mary had regained some of her composure by now

and she sat down again. She had the upper hand now and she intended to keep it. "I would like my thousand dollars, in cash as usual, at five o'clock tomorrow night."

"Do you want the bank notes perfumed before delivery?" Kearie asked sourly.

Mary did not bother to answer him. She said, "Is that understood?"

Sebree was watching her with sober attention. "This is your last demand, of course," he said dryly, "or do you reserve a woman's privilege of changing her mind?"

"Yes, it's the last. I'm just getting it while you've got it, Sebree. Or can you write checks in jail?"

Deyo said fretfully, "I wish you wouldn't keep saying that."

Sebree said slowly, "I'm willing to pay this time if I had some assurance that you wouldn't take the newspaper straight to Welling after you had collected the money."

"Did I before?" Mary countered.

Sebree's gaze was searching. "No. But before, you didn't claim to see the end in sight. Now you do. Is that because you intend to bring the end yourself?"

"You'll have to take my word for it that I'm not. Once you're in jail, I'll burn the paper."

"Don't say that!" Deyo's voice was high and almost hysterical.

Mary stood up, looked at Deyo and said, "Poor little man! You've been a nice puppy to Sebree. I wonder if the government will have a special kennel for you?"

She glanced at Sebree then. "Tomorrow night," she reminded him.

Sebree nodded. Neither of the three men stood up as she walked across the room and let herself out, closing the door behind her.

After she had gone, there were long seconds of gloomy silence. Deyo and Kearie watched Sebree. He puffed unhurriedly on his cigar, frowning in concentration.

Kearie burst out, "Damn the day she found that newspaper!"

"Stole it, you mean," Deyo said sourly.

Sebree glanced over at Deyo and said quietly, "You're doing her an injustice, Ross. She's a nice tough-minded girl. She's no petty thief."

"What's petty about the money she's got from us?"

Sebree smiled, "I take the 'petty' back. But she's no thief."

"Well, damn the day anyway, no matter what she is!" Kearie said. "Albers could have kept it for a year and would still have been scared to use it. I wish he had it now."

Sebree said softly, "I don't."

The two men regarded him with an expression of puzzlement on their faces. Kearie finally asked, "Why not?"

"Albers was the kind who would hunt up a man tougher than he was to blackmail us, and then claim a split of the profit. We are lucky we are dealing with a woman."

When neither man answered, only looked at him as if he had uttered blasphemy, he smiled slightly. "We'll have that paper back."

Deyo said, "When we're all flat broke, sure!"

"We'll have it back soon and without paying any more money for it," Sebree stated.

Kearie and Deyo watched him a morose minute, disbelief in their faces. Sebree looked from one to the other and then his glance settled on Deyo. "Ross, were you listening carefully when she threatened to turn over the paper to Welling if anything happened to Dixon?"

Deyo nodded.

"How carefully?" Sebree insisted.

"Why—she was mad," Deyo said. He frowned as he tried to recollect her words.

"No, she wasn't," Sebree said softly. "She was scared."

"Of what?" Kearie asked.

Sebree spread his hands, "Of what might happen to Dixon. Are you blind? She loves the man." He looked at each of them as they considered this.

It was Kearie who spoke first. "Suppose she does? How does that get us the paper? She'd give it to him if she were going to give it to anybody."

Sebree leaned back in his chair and sighed, "You're thick, Kearie. So are you, Deyo. Good God, how plain does it have to be?" Now he thrust forward in his chair and spoke earnestly to them both. "All we have to do is get hold of Dixon and keep him; then let her ransom him back with a copy of the newspaper!"

He waited, watching the vast relief flood into the faces of his confederates. Finally Kearie threw back his head and laughed. Just as suddenly he sobered and said glumly, "I don't know why I'm laughing. That won't put out my paper tomorrow."

Closing the door behind him, Giff lighted the lamp on his dresser, then crossed to the window and opened it. The imprisoned heat of the day began to escape from the room as he moved over to his bed and, sitting on the edge of it, pulled off his boots. Rising, he unstrapped his shell belt and hung it over the back of the chair beside his bed. Then, yawning widely, he stripped off his shirt. He was hanging it on the chair back when the hushed knock came at his door.

Reaching for his gun, he said, "Come in," and watched the door open quickly. A tall puncher in work-soiled clothes slipped into the room and, with one last look into the hall, closed the door behind him and regarded Giff.

"You still want that newspaper?" he asked.

Giff's heart gave a leap of excitement. "Have you got it? The April seventeenth issue of last year?"

The puncher nodded, "Good as. My old pappy found a copy."

"Where is it?"

"Why—home," the puncher said. A crooked grin broke the surface of his unshaven face. "You don't think I'd bring it with me. There's three Torreon hands watching the lobby now."

Giff said, "Then they know you are here, don't they?"

The puncher shook his head. "Not me. I took a look into the lobby and then come up the back way."

Cass's prediction had been fairly accurate, Giff thought. People were afraid to approach Welling, knowing Sebree would be watching him. Giff regarded the man before him in silent judgment. He did not like the looks of the puncher; he was needlessly dirty and was uneasy under Giff's close examination. But this was no time for judgment. If the man had the paper that was all that was necessary. "Where do you live?"

"Florence Creek, four miles west."

Giff hesitated, a wariness he could not define making him reluctant to move. He said presently, "Welling advertised for the paper. Why didn't you hunt him out?"

The puncher was shaking his head before Giff had finished, "Huh-uh. He'd get drunk and tell Sebree who sold him the paper."

"What's Sebree got to do with it?" Giff prodded.

Again the puncher's sly grin came and vanished, "It's all over town that something in this paper will mean jail for Sebree. Isn't that right?"

Giff didn't answer. He asked abruptly, "What's on the front page of that issue?"

"Besides April 17, 1882? I don't know; I didn't look."

This was the time to act and yet Giff did not move toward his shirt. The man's answers were reasonable enough. It was only his appearance that Giff mistrusted. *What should he look like?* he asked himself in sudden disgust. The man had the paper he wanted.

He moved over and picked up his shirt and climbed into it, then pulled on his boots. The puncher, suddenly uninterested in him, had moved to the door and had his ear to it, listening. The man's transparent fear of discovery was somehow reassuring.

Giff picked up his hat and considered his next move. It would be dangerous to take out a livery horse, since undoubtedly the livery was being watched too. He surprised the puncher regarding him with an alert curiosity. "I brought a horse, if that's what's worrying you," the man said. "He's tied at the edge of town."

A kind of balkiness he realized was foolish made Giff want to probe further; this was what he had suffered and sweated and fought for, yet when it was offered to him he had to examine it like he would a horse that seemed too much of a bargain. Wanting more time, he asked irrelevantly, "What makes you think I won't tell Sebree you sold me the paper?"

"You don't know my name, and you won't. I don't even live on Florence Creek. You'll wait for me at a crossroads outside of town. I'll get the paper and give it to you when you give me the money."

Good man, Giff thought, and his suspicion died. He asked, "Down the back way?"

The puncher nodded. "Suit yourself, but I think that's best."

Giff signaled him to open the door. The man palmed it open slowly and took a long look up and down the hall before he stepped out. Giff patted his hip pocket and felt the wallet containing the government's fifty dollars that Welling had given him.

He moved out into the hall, closed the door gently behind him and followed the puncher down the dim-lit corridor. At a cross passage the man turned left, and Giff saw the door of the fire escape still open. The puncher halted and said, "That stair rail is loose. Better keep close to the building." Then he vanished into the night.

Giff stepped outside and felt for the first step. Once he found it, he followed the man's advice and began the descent of the steps. Slowly his eyes accustomed themselves to the pitch black night; a diffused light from town barely illuminated the puncher's figure as he hit the alley, paused a moment to make sure Giff was following, then walked around the corner of the hotel, headed for the alley mouth.

Unconsciously Giff hurried the last few steps and took the corner at a half run. He saw the waiting men too late and knew he was trapped. The gun barrel aimed and moving for his head in a down falling arc was too swift to dodge. He felt only a blinding pain and then nothing.

6

WHEN THE stage pulled out of Taltal in a thunder across the bridge, Bentham turned back into the deserted bar. He glanced at the Mexican woman cleaning up the last of the dishes from the big trestle table in the dining room and then went on to the bar to take care of his own small chores.

This was the night he was going. He had given it much thought and had concluded the way to do it was quietly, without letting Sarita know he was leaving. As he rinsed out the glasses and put them on the back bar, he realized this was the last time he would do it. In another hour, as soon as Sarita was asleep, he would take a horse from the corral and leave, heading first for Taos and then south to the border. He was unused to horses and the ride to Taos was not an enjoyable prospect for him but the stage was too open, and he had rejected it.

He busied himself about the bar counting out all its and the hotel's cash and pocketing it. If Dixon had given him more time, he could have quietly sold every building, all the stock and every stick of furniture on the place. As it was, he thought sourly, he was leaving only with pocket money.

When he heard the Mexican woman close the back door on her way home, he moved over and blew the overhead kerosene lamps out. He wanted no late customers tonight. Picking up the lamp from the dining room table, he tramped upstairs and down the corridor to his sparsely furnished room.

From under his bed he drew out a folded duffel bag. For a neat man the prospect of putting clean clothes into a sack to be tied behind his saddle was not a pleasing one, but even he knew a suitcase was too awkward to handle on horseback. He set about packing his few belongings into his duffel bag. It was a leisurely process and occasionally he paused and looked out the window into the night. The big building was utterly quiet, save for an occasional creak of the roof timbers cooling off from the day's sun.

Oddly and against his will he felt a reluctance to leave this place. Such as it was, it had been his home for two years. Its quiet had never palled on him and he supposed that was because he was getting to be an old man. The thought that again he would have to make his meager living in a world of younger men was almost frightening. The border towns were best, even if they were poorer. His age and the fact that he was an American would be in his favor among the illiterate, hard-drinking Mexican gamblers. It wasn't much to look forward to, he admitted wryly to himself, but it could be a living if he was careful. Anything was worth it, as long as Sebree got what was coming to him.

He was standing before his bureau drawer trying to choose five shirts from the dozen and a half lying before him when he heard above the clatter of the creek the sound of a trotting team and the rattle of iron tires on the rough canyon road downstream. Quickly he moved to the lamp and blew it out. Then he came back to the window and stared out into the dark. Presently, he distinguished the sound of two other horses besides the team. They made a tremendous racket as they crossed the bridge and pulled up in front of the saloon where, screened by the black night, they halted.

Someone bawled, "Bentham! Bentham!" in an irritable voice and he recognized with a sudden feeling of guilt the voice of Traff. Had Sebree discovered his treason already? He thought carefully and because his whole life had been a gamble, he gambled now. Poking his head out the window, he called, "What is it?"

"Open up! Get some light in the place!" Traff's voice still held a truculence.

Bentham struck a match, pulled out his handkerchief

to hold the still hot chimney, lit the lamp and went downstairs with it. Placing it on the bar, he unlocked the saloon door, then came back and lit the overhead lamps.

Outside, there was a grunting commotion and the stamping of heavy boots on the porch which he could not understand until Traff came through the door. Three men followed him carrying the body of a fourth man between them. Bentham, with a small sense of shock, barely recognized Traff at first, although his squat thick body could not be mistaken for anyone else's. It was his face that was different; the whole right side of it was swollen and purple and his eyes, bleared and pain-racked, were barely open. He looked, Bentham thought, as if he had fallen headfirst down a mine shaft.

Traff said in a rough voice, "Dump him on the floor," and walked straight for the bar, saying, "Whiskey, Bentham; hurry it up."

But Bentham stood motionless, regarding the man the Torreon hands slacked to the floor.

It was Dixon, dirty, bloody and bound.

For long seconds Bentham looked at him, trying to still the panic rising within him. This was the man in whose hands he had placed his very life. As Bentham moved over to the bar, he was certain that Dixon had not betrayed him, else Traff's greeting would have been different. His still, contained face was expressionless as he set a bottle and shot glass in front of Traff but his pulse was pounding.

Traff irritably pushed the shot glass aside and said, "Give me a water glass."

Bentham took one from the back bar and watched Traff half fill it with whiskey and gulp it down.

When Traff had recovered his breath, Bentham said, "What happened to you?"

"I've about a yard of bailing wire holding a broken jaw together," Traff said sourly. "It hurts to talk, so don't ask questions."

He wheeled from the bar and went over to the three Torreon hands standing over Dixon. Bentham briefly

examined the three and knew that this was trouble.
Two of them were young and wild-faced men, barely
older than boys. They were the kind of reckless, tough
trash that Sebree paid well and kept in Torreon's most
isolated line camps, men who were good for just two
things—for night riding that left dead men in its wake
and for protection against retaliation for their night
riding.

Traff said, "Stand him up." A man grabbed each of
Dixon's arms and hauled him to his feet, facing Traff.
Blood and dust matted Dixon's hair and he had a sick
whiteness about his mouth. The hatred in his dark eyes,
however, was a shining thing that chilled Bentham.

Without so much as a word of warning, Traff spread
his feet and savagely drove his fisted hand into Dixon's
belly.

Dixon jackknifed and Traff, moving in to him, lifted
a knee into Dixon's face. It was quick and final. Dixon
slumped to the floor and lay motionless. Traff regarded
him thoughtfully, then kicked him in the head. Dixon
did not move, and the three Torreon hands watched
Traff with a kind of disinterested curiosity to see if
more would follow.

Traff turned and beckoned Bentham to him. If it
was coming at all, it would be now, Bentham knew;
but he moved up to Traff with total unconcern in his
face.

"You got an attic in this place?" Traff asked. When
Bentham said he did, Traff said, "Show me."

Bentham led the way upstairs. At the far end of the
corridor was a trap door in the ceiling. Access to it was
by way of a ladder raised to the ceiling by sash weight
and pulley. Bentham pulled the ladder down and while
Traff held it, he climbed up and lifted the trap door
back into the attic. Traff climbed up behind him and
thumbed a match alight, looking about him. The pitch
of the roof was steep against the heavy mountain snows
so that the attic was roomy; it had no windows and
only the small holes under the heavy-ridge timber provided ventilation. A few planks were stretched across
the joists and on them were two trunks, both open, a

stack of empty bushel baskets, a rusted axe and two shuck mattresses soiled beyond use.

Traff grunted, walked the planks to the trunks, looked in to make sure they were empty, picked up the axe and then the match died. The close, stifling heat of the room almost gagged Bentham. Traff struck another match and then motioned Bentham to precede him down the ladder. Once in the corridor, Traff leaned the axe against the wall and said, "That'll do."

"It'll fry him in the daytime," Bentham said quietly.

"Good." Again Traff thumbed Bentham into motion. Sarita, who was standing in the doorway of her room, a blanket around her, looking at them, vanished silently, closing the door behind her. Neither Traff nor Bentham indicated that he had noticed her.

Down in the saloon once more, Traff asked for a lantern. When Bentham brought one from the kitchen, Traff directed the three men to carry Dixon to the attic, and he followed their unsteady progress up the stairs and up the ladder. Bentham lagged behind, watching, his mind in a turmoil of conjecture.

Before the three men had descended from the attic, Traff opened the door of the closest room, went inside and came out with a straight-backed chair which he set in the corridor at the foot of the ladder and against the wall. When the three Torreon hands were once more in the corridor, Traff gave his directions.

"One of you sleep; the other sit in that chair. If he gets out of there, you're dead, both of you." Traff beckoned the third man and then walked down the hall to confront Bentham. "I'm going. Feed them, and him too." He said over his shoulder, "Come on, Barney," went on down the stairs and out of the saloon.

Descending the steps, Bentham heard the buckboard and one saddle horse move across the bridge and down the canyon.

He locked the saloon door and then moved over to one of the tables, drew out a chair and slowly sat down. Tiredly, almost stupidly, he stared at the walls of the room; but his thoughts were in a wild and jumbled tangle.

I'm trapped, he thought bleakly. He couldn't leave now without arousing suspicion, and surely under further beating Dixon would talk. His own treason would be part of that talk. With a galling bitterness he recalled his previous judgment of Dixon as the man who would down Sebree. What insane impulse had prompted him to confess to Dixon his hatred of Sebree that night? And why had he thought that Dixon, only an ordinarily tough but lucky man, was something special? There was nothing special about him tonight as he lay bloody and helpless and beaten.

Drawn by the magnet of self-pity, his thoughts returned to his own predicament. He couldn't leave here and he couldn't stay. The only thing he could do was sit tight, play out his hand and hope to dodge what was coming. Rising with a sigh, he blew out the lights and went upstairs toward uneasy sleep.

Next morning Sarita greeted him in the kitchen with a kind of cautious neutrality. When the cook was in the dining room, Sarita asked, "What went on last night?"

Bentham shrugged, "My orders are to feed them."

"Two of them?"

Bentham eyed her coldly, "Dixon's locked in the attic."

Sarita held his gaze a moment, then looked away. *She's Grady's all right,* he thought. *She's even scared to ask questions.*

He hung around the dining room until Sarita came out with a loaded tray. Intercepting her as she headed for the stairs, he said, "Put a pitcher of water on that," and took the tray. When she had fetched the water, he carried the tray upstairs and down the corridor.

One of the Torreon hands, ringed by a circle of ashes and cigarette butts, sat with his chair tilted back against the wall. At Bentham's approach, he rose and said, "I'll take that to him."

Bentham eyed him coldly, "Get out of the way, son."

The young puncher backed up a step but he was not giving away, Bentham knew. He only wanted room for anything that could happen.

Bentham took a chance then. He said dryly, "I knew

Sebree when you had to climb a fence to get on a pony. Now get out of my way and pull that ladder down."

The younger man said softly, "Pull it down yourself, Pop." But he went back to his chair.

Bentham set the tray on the floor, pulled the ladder down, held it with his foot and ascended to the attic. The light here was dim and he could barely make out the form of Dixon lying on the shuck mattress. Walking over to him, he halted and said, "Are you awake?" in a low voice.

"Put it down," Dixon whispered hoarsely.

As Bentham knelt to put the tray beside him, Dixon said in the same soft bitter voice, "You got a gun on you?"

"No."

"How many down there?"

"Four," Bentham lied.

"Bring me a gun next trip."

"What does he know about me?" Bentham asked.

"Nothing," Dixon whispered. "Don't worry. Just get me a gun."

Bentham rose and looked down at him for long seconds, "Are you too hurt to handle one?"

"I'll handle it. Just get it to me."

Bentham said all right and turned and descended through the trap door. To the puncher seated below, he said in passing, "Wake your friend and then one of you come down to breakfast."

He did not go downstairs, but went to his corner room and softly closed the door. It was only rarely that Bentham smoked, but now he went over to his dresser, took from its top drawer a sack of tobacco and neatly rolled a thin cigarette and lighted it. Then he sank into the rocking-chair, put his feet on the bed and stared thoughtfully at the wall. This was his moment of choice. He could get a gun to Dixon with no difficulty. *But should I?* he wondered. His whole future lay in how he would answer that question.

Suppose he got the gun to him. Dixon could kill one of his guards for certain, and with any luck, the other; but what Dixon would do afterward was what was deeply troubling Bentham. If he read Dixon's character rightly, Dixon would make a try for Sebree. It would be a wild, reckless and deadly try. *But will it work in time to save my hide?*

For long minutes Bentham considered this with a dismal foreknowledge of what his answer would be. He was a gambler by profession, he reflected, and he should be expert in assessing odds. What were Dixon's chances of success? *About forty to one,* he thought.

It was at that moment that Bentham knew the answer. A man was a fool to gamble at those odds. A young and reckless man might, but he was old and tired. *And afraid,* he thought calmly. *I've always been afraid, and I still am.*

He lost track of the time he spent in pondering this. Only a sharp knock on his door brought him into the present. Rising, he moved over and opened the door to find the same cold-faced young guard standing before him .

"He wants you to bring him another pitcher of water, Pop."

This was his last chance, Bentham knew. He could make his gamble and take the gun up to Dixon.

"All right, *you* take him one," Bentham said, and he closed the door.

When he came downstairs an hour later, he complained to Sarita of a toothache. By noon, he was groaning in his room so that the Torreon hands could hear him.

By that evening, his cheeks were pouched out with wadded paper and he reeked of oil of cloves. Nobody thought it strange, least of all the two Torreon hands, that he should take the stage that night to Taos and a dentist.

Cass put up his tools in a corner of the livery office and then with only mild regret at leaving his farm, faced the day's work. Sitting down at his desk, he fumbled around among the litter of papers, found a stub of pencil and, after some hunting, an envelope whose back was not scribbled on. Tilting back in his chair, he began to make a list of things he must do that day. There were oats to order and he'd be lucky if he found any between here and Vegas. There were two rental saddles that had to be taken to Burts for repairs. Who was it that had promised him a pair of kittens to help out old Benny, the stable Tom, with his mousing?

He was trying to remember this when, through the long-unwashed front window, he made out the figure of Fiske turning into the runway of the livery. Fiske halted at the door, said good morning and came in. Cass, glad of any interruption that would get a pencil out of his hand, threw his list on the desk and watched Fiske sink into one of the chairs by the door. Fiske was wearing his duck jacket and ancient derby but he had forsaken the laced boots today in favor of a pair of flat-heeled, wide-toed, and heavy farmer's shoes that Cass silently admired.

"Seen Giff this morning?" Fiske asked.

"Nope. Are you after horses?"

Fiske shook his head and said idly, "Not today; to-morrow maybe." He crossed his leg and felt gingerly the spot on his cheek where he had shaved too closely that morning. "It's town work today."

Cass laced his fingers, placed his hands on the back of his neck, tilted his chair back, swung his feet to the desk top and asked curiously, "What do you people find to do in town? Just peck at Deyo?"

Fiske smiled fleetingly. "No, it's mostly dull stuff. This morning I'll spend with the county clerk looking over the list of deeds recorded the last couple of years. Maybe for a drink and a cigar, the clerk will tell me which deeds were recorded by Sebree's men."

"I doubt that," Cass said.

"So do I." Fiske grinned again. "Funny how scared these county people are when you go to check on anything of Sebree's. They know damn well you'll find what you're after anyway, but it's surprising how short their memories for names and dates are."

"Not surprising," Cass growled. "They know who feeds them. Torreon does and Welling doesn't."

Fiske grunted agreement.

"How is Welling making out with Torreon?" Cass asked.

Fiske shrugged impatiently, "All right, I suppose. But as big as Torreon is, the way Sebree has covered his tracks and the way he's trained his boys to disappear at sight of us, I might as well buy a horse here."

Cass said nothing and the two men fell silent. Cass, looking out the window saw a passerby halt, then remove his hat and face the street. Curiously Cass came out of his chair, passed Fiske on his way to the runway. Fiske, curious too, rose and followed him out.

Coming down Grant Street was a black and dusty hearse followed by four or five buggies and surreys filled with mourners. The two men watched the procession until it was abreast of them and then they, too, briefly removed their hats.

"Who's that?" Fiske asked after it had passed.

"Old codger named Miles, a clerk over at Edwards," Cass replied. "Shot himself the other night. Funny thing," he went on musingly, "he used to own Edwards' store, but his real business was bucking the tiger at Henty's. Joe Henty wound up with his store finally, and Edwards bought it from him for a dime on the dollar. This fellow went back to work as a bookkeeper in his own store and he's never missed a night at Henty's since."

Fiske said without much interest, "That's the way it goes."

They talked a few moments longer about nothing in particular and then Fiske headed across the road toward the Plains Bar. *To pick up Welling,* Cass thought.

Cass went back to work. Before he was seated he suddenly remembered who promised him the kittens; along with that came memory of the small chore Giff had asked of him yesterday. Out in the stable, he picked up the two saddles, swung one over each shoulder and tramped down the alley, headed for Burts. After he had deposited them there, he walked up Grant Street in the warm midmorning sunshine. The sight of Welling and Fiske leaving the Plains Bar reminded him of Giff; he wondered if Giff had succeeded in placing the new reward notice in the paper that was to be out to-day. He doubted it, although Dixon was a lucky man. *Or is it luck?* Cass wondered. One thing sure, if Welling ever finished his investigation with solid proof that the government could use to prosecute Sebree and Deyo, it would be thanks to Dixon alone.

On the hotel steps Cass paused for a word with a rancher he knew from Isbell Canyon way. As he talked, he noticed the sign on the door of Edwards' store across the street. Even at this distance, Cass could read, "Closed for funeral." There was a bow of black satin tied to the door handle.

He crossed the lobby and went up to the desk. Arch Newson, the clerk, was a man Cass did not like and seldom bothered to speak to. Without greeting him, Cass turned the big ledger, which served as a hotel register and lay open on the desk, so that he could read its open pages.

Newson said, "Expecting somebody?"

"Uh-huh," Cass said not looking up. "Drummer for an implement company."

"What's his name?"

"That's it, I've forgotten. If I see it, I'll remember it." With a small feeling of pleasure Cass saw the name of James Archer on the register at the tail of the list. He murmured, "Archer—Archer—No, that's not it. What's this Archer look like?"

"He's no drummer," Newson said disdainfully. Then he frowned and thought. "Funny thing," he said, "damned if I remember what he looks like. Cowman, though."

Cass thanked him and went out. On the plankwalk he halted, remembering Giff's further request. He supposed there was no immediate hurry to tell Giff of Archer's presence but now that the man was here, Cass began to speculate in earnest as to Giff's whereabouts. He wondered if it had occurred to Fiske to look in Giff's room.

Backtracking through the lobby, Cass climbed the stairs to the second floor and halted far down the corridor before the door of room nine. He knocked and,

receiving no answer, tried the door handle. The door
was unlocked and Cass poked his head inside the room.
The bed blankets were in mild disarray but the bed had
not been slept in. What next caught his attention was
the lamp on the dresser. It was alight.

For a puzzled moment Cass considered this, gently
closing the door, and then he started downstairs. It was
obvious Giff had left the room last night and had not
yet returned. For a fleeting moment Cass wondered if
Giff might still be in one of the saloons. It had happened to him a couple of times that late at night he had
placed the change from his last drink on a bet in a
gambling game only to find that he had started on a run
of luck lasting well into the next morning. According-
ly, he tramped down to the Plains Bar, found it almost
deserted, with no games in progress, and moved on to
Henty's. Giff was not there.

Cass moved across the street and had a cup of coffee
at the Family Cafe but memory of Giff's room kept
teasing at him. What had started out as innocent speculation was becoming a mild obsession. If Fiske was
surprised enough at Giff's absence to ask his whereabouts, it meant that he was not on a land office errand. Cass speculated on who else in town would know
anything of Giff's movements and he thought immediately of Mary Kincheon. So far as his own present
knowledge went, Mary was the last person Dixon saw.
Perhaps he could trace his movements from there.

He finished his coffee and went downstreet to the
Free Press office. Stepping inside from the sunlit street,
he halted in astonishment, his hand still on the door.
Earl Kearie had cleared the big desk under the window
of all its papers. Atop the desk was a foothigh pile of
metal slugs that Cass only belatedly identified as type.
Kearie was seated in a chair at the far side of the desk,
beside him was an empty type stand. His coat was off
and in his left hand he held a large magnifying glass;
in his right was a piece of type. Propped against the
window were two big type charts to which he was re-
ferring when Cass entered. Kearie's expression, always
surly, was one of wrathful exasperation. He glanced at

Cass and then through the glass at the piece of type he held in his fingers.

Cass asked, "What's the matter? Are they dirty?"

Kearie said almost snarling, "What do you want?"

"Mary Kincheon."

"I fired her!" Kearie said in a shout of anger. "I don't know where she is and I don't give a damn!"

A sudden calculation came into his face as he looked at Cass and asked almost civilly, "Can you set type?"

Cass shook his head in negation.

"Do you know anybody in town that can?" Kearie persisted.

Again Cass shook his head.

Kearie, with a gesture of disgust, threw the reading glass on the pile of type and shoved his chair back. He started to rise, then settled back in his chair, put both hands on his knee and regarded the pile of type with a lost and baffled look.

Cass asked, "Where's your printer?"

Kearie winced visibly. "I've sent for one," he said shortly.

Cass looked at the heaping pile of type and was still uncertain as to what Kearie was attempting to do. "Why've you got all this stuff up here?" Cass asked. "Don't that belong back there in the shop?"

Kearie's look was murderous. He said, "You run your stables and let me run my newspaper."

"This is your press day, isn't it?" Cass asked shrewdly.

His question seemed to move Kearie to a decision. Kearie rose, put on his coat, clapped his black hat on his bony skull, booted the type stand aside and started for the door. Halfway there he halted and then returned to the desk. From a drawer on its near side, he lifted out a cube of cue chalk and slapped it into his vest pocket. Then turning to the door, he said harshly to Cass, "Step outside. I'm locking up."

Cass stepped outside, watched Kearie lock the door with a savage impatience and then head across the street toward Henty's saloon and its billiard tables. Turning, Cass went on down the street, headed for

Mrs. Wiatt's. Although he was uncertain as to what had happened at the *Free Press* office, memory of Kearie's wrath brought a smile to his face. Mary Kincheon had quit him. Over what, Cass could not guess, but with her leaving, Kearie's days of indolence were over. The whole town had wondered why she had worked for him in the first place and in the second place why she had tolerated the overwork and the drudging hours while he idled.

At Mrs. Wiatt's Cass rang the bell. Mrs. Wiatt answered the door and told him Mary was in the back yard drying her hair. Cass walked around the house and found Mary sitting on the grass in the bright morning sunlight, and he sat down beside her. Being both a gregarious and curious man, Cass's first impulse was to ask Mary why she wasn't at work, thus getting the whole story of her dismissal by Kearie. But he remembered his errand and after they had exchanged the time of day, he asked, "Have you seen Giff Dixon this morning?"

Mary was running her fingers through her long hair that was already curling; her hand halted and she looked sharply at him. "No. How do you mean have I seen him? Is he hurt or something? Or do you mean has he been in to see me this morning?"

"That's what I mean—the last," Cass said. At his answer, he thought he detected a kind of relaxation in her manner.

"I haven't seen him since yesterday morning," Mary said. There was a special alertness in her eyes as she watched him. "Why? Can't you find him?"

Cass said soothingly, "No. But it doesn't matter; he's around."

Mary said, "It's more than that. You wouldn't have come clear here if you expected to see him on the street. Has something happened, Cass?"

Cass hesitated only a moment, then told her of his search for Giff. He tried to seem unconcerned but it did not come off.

Mary listened soberly, a kind of alarm rising in her. She remembered Kearie's anger of yesterday and she thought immediately, *No, Kearie's afraid of him.* Memmory leaped back to the conference in Sebree's office and she remembered Sebree's smug words—*He'll be taken care of.*

She fought down a mounting panic and made herself consider this carefully. Her threat to expose Sebree if any harm came to Giff had been plain and unadorned. Sebree had understood it too. He wasn't the sort of man who would let dislike of a person wreck his fortunes. He would hate Giff, of course, but not enough to risk ruinous exposure.

Mary said, not believing it, "Maybe he has friends. Maybe he's just tired of town."

"He didn't take a horse." Suddenly an expression of surprise came into Cass's face. He looked sharply at her and then away.

Mary asked, "What are you remembering, Cass?"

Slowly Cass plucked a handful of grass, held it in his rough and callused palm and looked at it and then discarded it. "If he's gone and he didn't take a horse, maybe he took the night train. Can you give me one good reason why he should stay here?"

It was true, there was no good reason, Mary thought. He'd been picked up by Welling for a camp swamper with no responsibilities other than seeing to the horses and to feeding Welling and Fiske; but in the course of time, the whole burden of Welling's investigation had fallen on him. He had done the work and he had taken the beatings. Why shouldn't he decide in some lonely and discouraging hour of last night that it wasn't his fight and that he had had enough of it?

It was plausible but somehow Mary did not believe that either. She said, "No I can't, Cass, but you don't believe he left either, do you?"

"No," Cass answered in a low voice, "I guess I don't, but where is he?"

"I can't tell you, but he'll turn up. I just know it."

On that illogical and inconclusive statement, Mary took her stand. Cass, realizing that his visit had settled nothing and that he had only communicated his doubts and worries to her, came to his feet, a sudden discouragement within him, and took his leave.

Afterward she brushed her hair out, then went inside to her room. It was a big corner room across the hall from the parlor, the best in the house. Entering it, she closed the door behind her, wanting privacy.

She seated herself before the walnut vanity and began to do up her hair. The day had a strange Sunday-like quality about it and she realized it was because she was not working on a weekday—*on a press day,* she corrected herself. A year ago the thought of not working on a weekday would have terrified her. Now she didn't care. There was Sebree's money deposited safely in a Las Vegas bank to fall back on. *Blackmail money,* she thought, and for the first time naming it in her mind gave her a small feeling of shame.

It was a sensation foreign to her, and puzzled at it, she let her hands fall to her side and stared at herself in the mirror. Up to now, there had been no sense of guilt in her relations with Sebree. He was dishonest and a crook, and she had simply uncovered one facet of his crookedness that he could not afford to have known. The day she had found the two copies of the April seventeenth issue of the *Free Press* tucked behind some ink bottles on a shelf high over Perry Albers' cot in the back of the pressroom, she had counted the luckiest day in her life. Simple curiosity prodded her into examining them. When she found one issue contained six more final proof notices than the other, she compared them with the copy in the files. She copied down the names of the six extra entrymen and found in the courthouse records that they had deeded their homesteads to Sebree.

Staring at her image in the mirror now, she frowned, trying to recall what she had thought when Sebree's swindle was uncovered. She had thought first of all of revenge—of getting even with the man who had so subtly corrupted her father, who had flattered him and loaned him money and neutralized him, and finally watched him drown in liquor. Mingled with that desire

for revenge was a wild need to show that she was not
weak and soft like her father, but tough-minded and
hard. Last of all, she remembered, was the need for
money.

She could have taken the papers and sent them in to
the General Land Office as evidence of fraud, but there
was a better way to get even. That way was blackmail,
making Sebree pay her for silence, and always having
Sebree in her power. The money was welcome, and
Sebree could afford it. As for the ethics of it, weren't
Big Men stealing lands all over the West, sometimes
with the collusion of the Land Office itself? Her evidence wouldn't change this corruption, and she would
have been a fool not to demand money from the cor-
rupters.

But now she wasn't at all sure she had been right,
and she realized it was Giff Dixon who had bred that
doubt. Her feeling of guilt was closely tied to him, too,
for if she had turned over her copies of the *Free Press*
to him at first, she wouldn't be worried about him
now. And she was worried, she told herself; she was
slowly approaching panic. There was one thing she
must hold to, though, and that was the belief that
Sebree loved riches above revenge.

She busied herself the rest of the morning helping
Mrs. Wiatt. In the back of her mind all that afternoon was the coming meeting with Sebree at Deyo's
office where she would receive the last of her blackmail
money. Perhaps Sebree would let slip by a word or an
expression that he knew of Giff's whereabouts. A little
before five o'clock, the hour that was set for the meeting, she put on a fresh dress and afterward called to
Mrs. Wiatt and asked if she needed anything from the
store. Then she let herself out into the warm late afternoon and made herself stroll the few blocks to the land
office at a leisurely pace.

The land office, cool and shaded against the late
afternoon sun, was deserted save for the Mexican clerk
working at his desk. She saw Deyo through the open
door of his office and a faint blue haze of cigar smoke

betrayed Sebree's presence there too. Lifting the counter gate, she nodded to the clerk and entered Deyo's office.

Sebree rose at her entrance and courteously placed a chair for her, then moved over to the door. Mary, with her back to him, did not catch his glance at Deyo, nor the brief movement of his head.

Deyo rose, gathered some papers together, and said stiffly, "I've got to go over these with my clerk. Excuse me." He went out, trailing a faint odor of bay rum.

Sebree walked over to the chair Deyo had vacated and sat down. Looking over the desk, he complained mildly, "Why won't some men put an ash tray in their office."

Mary was watching him closely. He seemed in his usual serene spirits, she thought, and she found herself hating him again, not for his rich clothes, his fine cigars, nor for what he represented, but this time for his bland and affable front.

Sebree tilted back in his chair and regarded her a brief and friendly moment before he said, "I didn't bring any money and I'm not going to pay you any more. You've been on the merry-go-round long enough and now you're getting off."

The mildness of his words in contrast to their content was confusing for a moment. When Mary understood their full meaning, she felt a nameless excitement. She had often wondered how she would handle this very situation and had rehearsed it in her mind. Remembering, she rose and said coldly, "Suit yourself, Grady."

Sebree said quietly, "Don't be in such a hurry. You haven't heard all I have to say."

"I've heard enough."

"I think not. The second thing I have to tell you is that I want your copy of the *Free Press.*"

Mary stared unbelievingly at him, then she said tartly, "You can get it tomorrow by taking it away from Dixon. He will have it."

Sebree began to shake his head slowly from side to

side. "You're wrong about that. Dixon won't have it by tomorrow morning for the simple reason that I've got Dixon."

Mary stood utterly still, terror seizing her. Then she sat down and Sebree read the torment in her face and smiled.

"You've got Dixon?" Mary echoed slowly.

Sebree nodded. "Unhurt and very well guarded."

Mary waited many seconds before she could trust herself to speak. "What are you going to do with him?"

"Why, trade him to you," Sebree said in mild astonishment at her lack of perception. "You give me your copy of the *Free Press* and I'll turn him back to you unharmed."

"Yes!" Mary said quickly. "Yes! I'm willing."

Sebree smiled, and said, "At your house at nine, say." When she nodded, he could not resist a last thrust. "Maybe he won't have you, once he knows you are a blackmailer."

"Maybe," Mary said quietly.

7

GIFF HAD been sleeping when he was aroused by the trap door slamming back on its hinges. Carrying the lantern ahead of him, Traff stepped into the stifling attic and then moved aside to make way for Giff's two guards. They were carrying ropes and wordlessly they rolled him over on his face and bound his hands behind him. Then Traff motioned with his gun for him to stand.

Giff rose unsteadily to his feet; the hot fetid air of his prison was like a drug and he stared stupidly at Traff. His mind worked with difficulty and he knew that he should be concerned now with this new move, but the heat, his thirst, and the pain of his aching head, had robbed him of all vitality.

"You're too heavy to carry," Traff said curtly. "Walk down."

One of the guards slipped down the ladder and Giff, as he approached the trap door with its blessed current of fresh air, could see him waiting below in the dim light of the corridor lamp. Uncertainly and awkwardly he made his way down the ladder and then Traff prodded him down the stairs and into the empty saloon.

Save for his guard and Traff, there was no one about. He had never seen Bentham after his first appearance in the attic. The lamps were all burning brightly and he blinked against the unaccustomed light. He turned his head to ask for water and, out of the corner of his eye, saw Traff's movement.

Putting a booted foot in the middle of Giff's back, Traff shoved. Too late Giff saw him and then he was off balance. He fell heavily to the floor and tried to roll over on his back in time for Traff's attack, but Traff approached him slowly and looked down at him.

"Want another kick?" Traff asked.

"Another won't matter," Giff said quietly. He knew Traff saw the cold, sustained hatred in his eyes, and he didn't care.

Traff only turned to the guards and said, "Tie his feet."

When that was done and his hat mashed down on his head, three of them lugged him out into the night and down the steps. He was thrown in a waiting buckboard and a tarp pulled loosely over him. Then began the long jolting journey. Giff had no idea of where he was being taken or for what reason. He could hear a horseman on either side of him, but there was no conversation. Sometime during the first half-hour, he heard the up-stage clatter full-tilt past them, raising such a racket that he could not have been heard even had he shouted.

Later they left the sound of the creek and achieved a smoother and less rocky road. Were they headed for Torreon, Giff wondered? For the past twenty-four hours, he had tried to fathom the reason behind his kidnaping and had not succeeded. He was fairly certain that if they intended to dispose of him as they had disposed of Albers, they would have done it by now. A lifeless body was much easier to haul along mountain roads and dim trails to its final resting place than a live man with a voice. The anger at his own gullibility the night he was seized had never ceased rankling. Beyong it was the deep and murderous hatred of Traff. Either Traff must kill him or he would kill Traff, and he wondered if the man knew that.

More than two hours had passed, he judged, when the buckboard and its outriders slowed from a mile-eating trot into a walk. In some way the sounds of the wagon tires and the hoofbeats were altered and seemed almost muffled. Giff listened closely, his senses alert, trying to interpret the change. Their pace slowed and finally they came to a halt.

"Everything all right?" Giff identified the voice as Sebree's. He heard Traff's voice say, "Sure," and then the sound of the two guards dismounting.

The canvas was yanked off him and above him he saw great arching trees against the night sky. His feet were grabbed and he was hauled halfway out of the buckboard, then raised to a sitting position. Immediately he saw he was in town and then, only an instant later, that the buckboard was pulled up in front of Mrs. Wiatt's.

A quick alarm came to him. What had Mary to do with any of this? He heard Traff's surly voice beside him in the dark. "Open your mouth and I'll belt your teeth out. Get down!"

Giff slipped to the ground and one of his guards undid the rope binding his feet while the other steadied him. He could make out Sebree's tall form standing by the gate before Traff's gun prodded him into movement. Abreast of Sebree he halted and said, "What are we doing here?"

Sebree laughed softly and said, "Go inside and find out." Sebree pushed past and they followed him up onto the porch where he rang the bell.

The door was opened immediately by Mary. She stood motionless only long enough to identify Giff. He could barely see a smile on her face at sight of him and he did not speak, only looked at her in a puzzled way that seemed to remind her of the others. She stepped aside and said, "Come in." The neat parlor was brightly lit and as they entered, Sebree was the only one to remove his hat. Giff was watching Mary for a clue to the cause of this strange meeting; she was excited and nervous, Giff saw, and oddly there was a happiness in her expression, too.

She came up to him and touched him and said, "My room is across the hall, Giff. Go in there for a minute."

Giff glanced from her to Sebree, who was regarding them with an amused tolerance. "No," Giff said. "What is this?"

"Please go, Giff."

"No," Giff said stubbornly. "Whatever's going on, I want to see it."

Mary turned her head to look at Sebree and the glance she exchanged with him meant nothing to Giff. He saw Sebree shrug, then heard him say to Mary, "I'll untie him if you want."

"Get those gunmen out of here first," Mary said coldly.

Sebree turned to his men. "Untie his hands and then get out on the porch by the door. Leave it open." The closest puncher released Giff from his bonds and then he, along with Traff and the other guard, moved out the door.

Sebree spoke to Mary now, "I have no gun with me, but I'll call them back if he moves." He shuttled his glance to Giff. "Is that understood?"

Mary only nodded and then turned and vanished into the dark dining room. Giff, totally bewildered by now, regarded Sebree with mounting suspicion and bafflement. "What are you doing here?" he asked.

Sebree said dryly, "I wouldn't spoil it for worlds."

Mary entered then and in her hand was a newspaper. She walked straight to Sebree and handed it to him. Sebree could not entirely conceal his haste to receive it and immediately he turned it over and read aloud, "April 17, 1882. That's the one I want." Then he discovered the second newspaper under the first. "What's this?"

"The true copy and the one Albers set up for Deyo," Mary said. "I did more than keep my word."

With a stunning force it came to Giff then what he was witnessing. Mary was trading the evidence that would ruin Sebree for his own freedom.

"No! Mary, no!" he shouted, and he moved instinctively toward her.

Sebree backed away saying sharply to Mary, "Make him behave!"

Swiftly Mary wheeled and barred Giff's way. "Be still! Be quiet!" she demanded sharply. Then she swiveled her head and still holding him, said to Sebree, "Get out!"

Sebree lunged for the door and was gone.

Roughly Giff seized Mary as if to move her aside and follow, a wild reckless anger upon him.

Mary said harshly, "Are you asking them to kill you?"

Giff checked himself and looked down at her and then slowly removed his hands from her shoulders. It was true; he was unarmed and now that Sebree had retrieved the evidence that would ruin him, he would cheerfully kill before letting it go.

Only now did the full implication of Mary's act come to him. He scrubbed his unshaved cheek with the palm of his hand and then laid his accusing glance on Mary. She was standing close to him, watching him with sober eyes.

"You had them all the time," Giff accused.

"Ever since I found them months ago," Mary agreed quietly. "I've been blackmailing Sebree with them."

Giff said nothing, only watched her.

"Say it," Mary invited bitterly.

Giff shook his head slowly. "You've said it all."

"Not all," Mary said miserably. "To say it all, I'd have to tell you how my father fawned on him. I'd have to explain to you how good I felt when I demanded money from him and got it. I'd have to explain to you how his money is a special kind of money, not like other money, because he gave it to me in fear."

There was no pity in Giff's face as he listened. He said with a bitter mockery, "I'm surprised you let them go when they were making money for you."

Mary flushed at his words, but she didn't answer.

"Why didn't you give them to me in the first place?"

"I asked myself that yesterday."

"Then what changed your mind?"

Mary gave him a searching look and then said, "You can ask that, but I don't have to answer it, do I?"

Giff shook his head in bewilderment, "You're a strange girl," he said bitterly. "You're hard at the wrong times and soft when you should be hard."

"Like tonight?"

Giff sighed, "Like tonight. Why couldn't you have kept the papers? Why couldn't you have told Sebree you'd turn them in to Welling if he didn't free me?"

"I could have done that," Mary said slowly and then she added in an almost inaudible voice, "I guess that's what I should have done."

Giff said bitterly, "Well it's too late now."

"Too late for a lot of things," Mary murmured.

They faced each other almost with defiance, then Giff said, "All it means is that I'll have to get them back."

Mary said nothing and Giff turned and walked out of the house. In the deep shade of a tree by the front gate, he halted and looked back through the open door. Mary was standing the way he had left her and for a baffled and uneasy moment he watched her. He knew he had been rough and unkind, and that he should return and admit it.

But his pride and his haste checked him, as he thought of Sebree's triumph. He moved then, and not back toward the house, his mind already scheming ahead.

An unreasoning and furious stubbornness was upon him now. First of all he must get hold of a gun. Then someway, anyway, he must get the papers back from Sebree. Passing Henty's saloon he glanced at the horses lining its tie rail; by the dim light of the saloon's lamps, he saw the Torreon brand on the hip of the horse closest to him. Halting, he moved over and saw a second and a third horse, both branded Torreon. Turning now, he moved over to Henty's window and looked into the crowded saloon. There was Sebree seated at one of the card tables with Deyo and Kearie. Traff and another man made up the five-handed game of poker that Sebree seemed to be enjoying. At the bar Giff saw his two guards in conversation with the trio of punchers Giff recognized as Torreon hands. There could have been other Torreon hands in the crowd; probably there were.

The sight of half Torreon celebrating sobered Giff. The thought of taking the papers away from Sebree seemed impossible now. Surrounded by the pick of his toughest men, Sebree could afford to linger over his cards. Giff knew that if he walked into Henty's, he would never make it half way to Sebree's table.

But turning away from the window, his black stubbornness returned. *I'm going to try it anyway.* He passed the land office and saw the lantern hanging in the livery archway ahead. Stepping into the office, he saw Cass seated at his desk reading an old *Stockman's Gazette*. At his entrance, Cass looked up and then pitched the magazine to the floor. "Where've you been?" Cass demanded.

"I'll tell you later," Giff said shortly, and then added, "Same old question—got another gun?"

Cass said softly, "Oh, oh!" and watched him a long moment. Then he rose and moved over to the wall. On the nail was a holstered gun and shell belt which Cass took down. He said, walking toward Giff, "This is my hostler's. Don't lose it."

While Giff was belting on the gun, Cass watched him soberly. "Need any help?"

Remembering the line up of Torreon riders in Henty's, Giff shook his head. This wasn't Cass's fight and Giff said, "Not this time."

He was turning toward the door when Cass said, "That fellow showed up."

Giff halted and looked at him, puzzlement in his dark, stiff face.

"Jim Archer. He showed up. He's at the hotel."

"Thanks," Giff said and stepped out into the runway. By the time he had reached the plankwalk, his pace was slowing and then he halted. The idea taking shape in his mind seemed an unlikely one, but as he stood there pondering it, memory of what Henty's held for him came to him again. *Maybe,* he thought.

Wheeling, he turned upstreet toward the hotel. At the desk he asked of the clerk, "Which room is Archer's?" and was told. Tramping up the stairs, there was scant hope in him and for a moment his impulse was to turn around and give up the idea; but he went on and tramped down the corridor to the room named him by the clerk and knocked on the door.

He heard movement in the room and then the door opened. Confronting him was a middle-aged, mild-looking man, dressed in clean range clothes. He was of ordinary size with colorless, clean-shaven features. A saddle of thinning black hair crossed his pale bald head. He might have been any barber in any town—faceless, pleasant, trusted.

Giff asked, "Did anyone get in touch with you yet?"

Archer shook his head slowly. Giff stepped in and closed the door behind him, leaning on it. "You know your job?"

Archer seemed to think that question not worth answering. He said, "I've been paid for it. Just show me the man."

Giff felt a sudden almost sickening hatred of the man. Beyond that he felt a dread of what he himself was about to do. Here was a killing contracted for and paid for; all that remained was for him to choose the man to be killed. He thought of Sebree's crew at Henty's. Neither his wrath, his cunning, nor his courage would get him past them to Sebree, whereas this little man would go unnoticed.

All that remained was for him to give the word. Yet he felt a deep reluctance within him. The murderous irony of the situation did not escape him, but appreciation of it didn't help. Cold reason told him that this was only simple justice to Sebree. Instinct told him that it was the wrong way. Again memory of Sebree's crew came unbidden to his mind, pushing him to his decision. *Right or not, that's the way it has to be,* he thought, and he moved into the room, making his voice coldly matter-of-fact. "Your man is sitting in Henty's saloon now. Do you know the place?"

"I had a drink there this evening," Archer replied in a mild voice.

"Good," Giff moved over to the bare bureau top and Archer watched him closely.

"Pay attention now," Giff said. "Here's Henty's

door." And then on the bureau top, he sketched out the location of Sebree's table. Then he said, "Your man is facing the door. He's ___ ___ ___ tall, well-fleshed and his full mustaches are turning gray. He's wea___ ___ ___ a black coat and a new dust-colored Stetson. He has dark eyes and a florid complexion. He wears a heavy gold ring on the fourth finger of his left hand; he'll be smoking a good cigar."

Archer listened alertly and, when Giff was finished, Archer nodded thoughtfully and moved over to the chair on the back of which hung his gun belt. This was Sebree's paid assassin and Giff had a fleeting admiration for Bentham's choice. There was nothing about the man's physical description to attract any notice at all. Whatever courage and desperation and depravity was in the man was buried out of sight in his neat, almost deprecating, appearance.

When he had his gun belt strapped on, he picked up his hat and asked, "Tonight?"

"For sure," Giff said flatly.

Archer nodded almost indifferently and stepped out, closing the door carefully behind him.

Giff stood motionless, looking at the door. He had made his decision and still did not like it. A kind of dismal anger was in him and he struggled with the impulse to wrench open the door and shout for Archer to come back; but the deep and rough certainty that this was the only way held him motionless. Presently he moved to the door and stepped out. He had no notion of how Archer was planning to escape afterward, but he hoped someone in the Torreon crew would kill this quiet, unassuming murderer before he could.

At the land office corner, he moved up the steps into the deep shadows of its entrance and waited. Presently he saw a man leading a horse come out of the alley, cross the street and disappear into the alley behind Henty's. Afterward, watching the alley mouth, he saw him come out of it, take to Henty's plankwalk and enter the saloon.

It was Archer. Giff waited a moment longer and then moved to the corner. In his mind's eye, he could see

Archer, perhaps buying a cigar, lighting it and then sauntering aimlessly through the packed gaming tables. He would linger a moment watching one of the other games and perhaps decline an invitation to sit in. Eventually, when he had located and identified his man, he would move by easy stages to Sebree's table. There would be no invitation to play here, but watchers, especially strangers, were always tolerated. By now Archer would have located the rear door and would have boldly planned his exit. He would—

The sound of a shot inside Henty's yanked Giff into awareness and movement. He crossed the street slowly at first and then when the first man boiled out of the door on the heel of several gunshots, he ran, lifting out his gun. At the batwing door of the saloon, he let a man past him and then stepped inside.

The room was in pandemonium. The more prudent gamblers had dived under the tables. Others were fighting for the front door. Traff, gun in hand, was smashing his way through overturned chairs and wildly shouting men, headed for the alley door. Behind him were Sebree's guards viciously clubbing aside anyone barring their way to the rear exit. Behind them were three other men shouldering through in Traff's wake. A cursing bedlam filled the room.

It was toward Sebree's table that Giff roughly elbowed his way. He saw Deyo and Kearie standing at the table looking down at the floor where three men were kneeling. Giff circled so that at his approach he would face Kearie and Deyo. and then he knelt beside the other three. He had his brief look at Sebree sprawled on his back on the floor, eyes open and unseeing, blood pooling under him and spreading slowly on his white shirt front.

Roughly Giff reached into Sebree's inside coat pocket and felt only a wallet. His glance lifted to Deyo and only now did Deyo identify him. Protruding from under the lapel of Deyo's coat was an edge of the telltale paper. Giff rose as Deyo was turning. Giff lunged over Sebree's body, grabbed Deyo's arm and roughly spun him around. He rammed his gun into Deyo's soft midriff with a violence that drove the breath from the older man. With his free hand, he reached into Deyo's coat pocket and hauled forth the papers, wheeling away so that Kearie and the others came within the arc of his leveled gun.

"Better run now, Deyo," he said softly. Then he backed up a step, lowered his gun, and moved toward the rear door, not turning his back.

He could hear shouts on the street and in the alley; he stepped quickly through the alley door and put his back to the wall of the saloon. Traff was in the alley mouth bawling directions across the street. From down the other alley came a scattering of gunfire.

As Giff moved, his foot touched an empty bottle, sending it rolling into the wall of Henty's saloon. At its soft, almost secretive tinkle, Traff wheeled. In the half-light of the alley he identified Giff.

In a blind unthinking rage, Traff raised his gun and running toward Giff brought it down club-like and fired. On the heel of his shot, Giff raised his gun and when Traff's bulk blacked out his sights, he pulled the trigger. Traff sat down as if some unseen hand had pulled him to the ground, wrapped both arms about his midriff and toppled over.

Giff moved past him into the road and crossed it quickly. There were men milling in the street before Henty's, talking and watching the door. Holstering his gun, Giff skirted them and turned at the land office corner.

A couple of men at a dead run almost ran into him and as he stepped aside, he saw others in the street heading toward Henty's. In front of the Plains Bar a handful of men stood before the door looking down street as if undecided whether the ruckus were worth watching.

"What's the shooting?" one man, his deal of cards still in his hand, asked Giff. Giff shrugged and shouldered past him. Welling, he was certain, would be inside and he moved into the saloon and halted. Some of the gaming tables were deserted. At the corner table Giff saw Welling and Fiske and he moved toward them.

Fiske, a cigar clamped in the corner of his mouth, was looking bored and irritable. Welling's sullen face, slack and heavy with his nightly ration of whiskey, was staring without interest at the men lining the bar.

Fiske saw Giff first and came half out of his chair; his movement attracted Welling's attention and then Welling saw him. Giff halted before the table and put down the two newspapers. He said to Fiske, "There they are, Bill. You'd better get them to a safe place."

A curious transformation took place in Fiske's face. The irritability gave place to a stunned amazement as he reached for the newspapers; when he read the dates, saw both copies were here, an expression of almost bitter reverence came into his Scot's face.

Welling swept them roughly from Fiske's hand and looked at the dates too. A look of alcoholic elation leaped into Welling's face. He smiled, and then tapped them, looking up at Giff. "They're the ones stolen from Albers?"

Giff nodded.

"Who had them?"

"Mary Kincheon."

A faint, crooked smile touched Welling's face. He was remembering Mary's treatment of him. He said softly, then, "We'll see what the district attorney can charge her with. It's got to be something."

For a brief moment, Giff stared at him. Then he reached for the papers, drew them gently from Welling's hand, and laid them before Fiske.

Then, without a word, he reached across the table, balled up Welling's shirt and hauled him roughly out of his chair. Still without a word, he hit Welling in the face with all his might. Welling was torn from his grasp. He sat down in the chair and then somersaulted completely out of it, slammed against the wall and sprawled on his face.

Giff, rubbing his knuckles, looked at Fiske. The old man rose, sighed, said simply, "It's great to be young," picked up the papers, tucked them in his pocket and started for the door without so much as a backward glance at Welling.

A crowd began to collect now around the table, and Giff turned and without answering their questions went outside. He turned upstreet, then, headed for Mrs. Wiatt's. Memory of his rough words to Mary again brought a small shame to him now as he thought of them.

The crowd around Henty's was swelling. He heard one man on the fringe of it say to his companion in answer to a question Giff hadn't heard, "Sure. He made it to the livery in the alley, and then I guess Murray's horses spooked his pony. It throwed him, and he fought it out with Torreon."

"Who was it?"

"Stranger."

So Archer had lost his gamble, just as Sebree had lost his. Again, Giff felt a stirring of guilt; it was not regret for the deaths of Sebree and Archer, but for the way he had been forced to bring them about. He skirted the milling crowd and went on up the lonely street. He felt drained of all anger, but his feeling of guilt at memory of Mary nagged at him, touching him again with remorse. He winced inwardly as he remembered his words to her—self-righteous and accusing words. Remembering how she had looked at him, he knew she would have preferred that he cursed her.

Lamps were still alight in the house as he turned in, mounted the steps and knocked on the door. Mrs. Wiatt answered it.

She peered closely at him in the dim light reflected from the parlor lamp, and then recognized him.

"Are you responsible for the crying that's going on in there?" she demanded. Her head nodded in the direction of Mary's room.

"I likely am," Giff admitted.

Mrs. Wiatt swung the door open. "Do something about it," she ordered tartly.

Giff moved past her through the parlor and into the hall. Pausing before Mary's closed door, he knocked. Presently he heard her bid him enter and he opened the door. She was emptying a bureau drawer of her clothes which she was placing on the bed. At sight of him, she straightened up, looking slim and sad and fiercely alone.

He could see she had been crying and she did not try to hide it from him. Closing the door behind him, he came across the room and rested both hands on the footboard of the big walnut bed. "It's a little late to say I was too rough, isn't it?"

Mary nodded assent and Giff, again touched with shame, looked down at his hands.

"Are you going to apologize for speaking your kind of truth?" Mary asked quietly.

Giff glanced up, puzzled at her words.

"I know," Mary continued, "you don't admire blackmail. You don't have to say it again."

Giff shook his head slowly. "I never meant to say it at all."

"You had a right to. I'm not a good person. You know that now."

Giff looked searchingly at her, then came around the end of the bed and halted before her.

"You think I am? Have you ever wondered how I caught the buckshot Doc Miller pried out of me?"

When Mary didn't answer, he said, "Three of us trail hands decided one day we'd been without money long enough. There was a bank in one of these little trail towns that the government used to pay off drovers. It was full of money, and we wanted it."

He paused, watching the interest stirring in Mary's eyes.

"Two of us wanted it, that is; the third one decided he could make more money by warning the bank. They were ready for us when we got off our horses at the bank corner. That's where I picked up the buckshot—just as I stepped around my horse." He waited a moment. "How does blackmail stack up beside that?"

"Not very tall," Mary said softly.

Giff regarded her soberly. "Maybe that's why I wanted so badly to play out my hand here. I got kicked and beat into doing something straight, and I wanted to finish it straight. I could see it all when you handed those papers to Sebree. If I talked rough, I felt rough."

"I'm glad it's no apology," Mary said quietly.

Giff smiled and shook his head. He reached out and took one of her hands in his and looked down at it. It was a small, strong hand, and the inerasable grime of printer's ink stained it faintly. The sight of it reminded him again that this was no soft and pampered girl, but a woman who had known work and poverty, and even fear. She was his kind of woman, where the other kind could never be. She understood without having to put it into words the small dishonesties, the angers, the wrong judgments and the longings for something better that he had found in himself. All that was nothing without the gentleness, and the gentleness he had seen for himself.

He nodded to the clothes on her bed. "On the move again?"

She nodded soberly.

"Can you afford two train tickets? Neither one of us owns a horse."

"Tickets to where?" Mary asked softly.

"A place in Wyoming way back against the peaks. I've passed it a dozen times. It's so far away from a town it's lost. We'll have to build a school for our kids."

"I can afford the money," Mary said gently. "Can you afford the time—the rest of your life?"

ABOUT THE AUTHOR

MEET THE DERBY MAN—
THE NEW WESTERN POWERHOUSE

**Look sharp, hit hard—
that's the Derby Man's style.
He's a fast-moving mountain of muscle
who throws himself into the thick of
the West's greatest adventures.**

**14185-6   THE PONY EXPRESS WAR
by Gary McCarthy $1.75**

The Pony Express—a grueling 2,000 mile race through hell. The pace and terrain are deadly enough but vengeful Paiute warriors and murdering saboteurs led by a sadistic giant threaten to turn the route into a trail of blood. Until one man has the brains and brawn and guts to save the Pony Express—The Derby Man.

**14477-4   SILVER SHOT
by Gary McCarthy $1.75**

It's hard-rock mining and rock-hard brawling as the Derby Man takes on a boom town. A man could mine fabulous wealth on the Comstock but the Derby Man strikes only a motherlode of trouble. With his sledgehammer fists and sharply honed wits he sets out to expose a spellbinding stock manipulator.

**These Derby Man adventures are available
wherever Bantam Books are sold.**

C

Presenting the exciting opening pages
of a powerful new frontier novel

A KILLER
COMES TO SHILOH
by C. H. Haseloff

Thunder splits the night as the Shiloh death bells
toll the frightening news—a mysterious killer
has brutally cut down three young lives...

The bells that had drawn Joshua Shank into the blackness of the storm were louder now. Hollow and grim came the sound from their iron throats.

In a flash of lightning Joshua saw the church doors with the death notes nailed upon them. Ducking his head against the rain that blew onto the uncovered porch, he climbed the stone steps. Three notes were tacked to the double doors. The torn edges of the papers flapped as fingers of wind slipped beneath and tore them. He held the lantern high, straining to read the words that washed from the wet pages. The window glass beside the door rattled in the wind.

Josh wiped the rain from his eyes. From the Cherokee script, with English below, he read:

> "Mary Louise Neil is dead forever. At a murderer's hand. She was a Christian ten years old. Now she has passed from the earth to the place of long rest, leaving behind anguish for the living. Now she has no pain."

The second and third notes were the same except for the names and ages of the children—Jo Belle Walker, age nine; Rebecca Ann Beard, age eight. Josh bent his head, pressing his eyes with his tough brown fingers. Tears mixed with the rain on his cheeks.

"Shank, come inside," Tom Bryan said. "Come out of the weather." Joshua followed him into the church. In the dim light he could see the shoulders of men in the front pews and hear the murmur of their words.

"We don't know it's true," Bob Little said thickly.

"Why would somebody put up something like that on a night like this?" a voice asked from the darkness of a pew.

"What better night for such news?"

"Why didn't whoever put up them notes stay

around? That's purty peculiar puttin' up the notes, ringin' the bell, then disappearin'. Like a joke or some- thin'." Pettigrew Wills still wore his house slippers. His nightshirt was stuffed into his britches. The red gal- luses and striped shirt looked gay and bright in con- trast to the dark world. "I was here in five minutes. Somebody done his work and left out the back before I could get here."

"Shank, do you figure it's a joke?" Tom Bryan asked.

"I don't know, Tom. Maybe we ought to check the campmeeting before we go any further."

"That's right. We ought to check," Sam Waters said. "Sure. Somebody ought to go out to the camp. All those girls' families were at the meeting. Saw 'em yesterday evening."

Nobody moved to leave the church for the storm.

"I'll go home and get dressed," said Wills. "And you and me can go out there, Shank."

"By the time you get dressed, Petti, we can all go out there and get back." Sam Waters wanted action. Wills' ways were too slow and ponderous.

"All right. All right. But we'll have to get our horses or a wagon or something. Damn, we're all on foot, and it's three miles out there," Wills said.

"Shank, take my horse," said Tom Bryan. "She's fast, and you're the best rider among us. You can get out there and find the truth before we get organized. Rest of you men go on over to the house. Clary'll have coffee ready by now. We can wait over there together."

Joshua followed Tom around the house and into the stable out back. The barn smelled musty like wet hay. Tom's sorrel mare whinnied at them. Tom Bryan acted as mayor of Shiloh. Like Joshua's family he had set- tled Shiloh when it was nothing more than some strung out farms along the Indian line. He'd started the first store.

"If it's true, Josh—" he thought a moment. "If it's true, we'll have to keep our heads. Folks'll take it mean. Whoever did it will go to the Nations to hide, probably. We'll wire Fort Smith for a marshall."

"Let's be sure first," Josh said, swinging into the saddle. "I'll be back as soon as I can, Tom." He kicked the mare, ducked the door jam and cantered into the rain.

Tom stood in the doorway a few minutes. He watched the other town men standing on his back porch holding coffee mugs. Clary'd have breakfast soon. "Killin's too good for a bastard who'd kill them children," he heard one of them say. "It'll be a pleasure stringin' him up." It had already begun—the quick, blind call of blood for blood.

A faint light was growing as Joshua rode into the meeting grounds. The camp was three miles from Shiloh and no one on the grounds had heard the bells through the storm. A few men were out driving tent stakes deeper and digging run-off trenches. Smells of bacon and coffee came from the women's area. Men could only enter there from an hour after sun-up until an hour before sundown. That was Reverend Poe's rule. The local preachers bowed to his wisdom. Camp meetings could confuse the feelings of believers. And sexual love might be mistaken for spiritual. So the men and women had separate, inviolate areas to insure high purpose.

The Shiloh campmeeting drew families from Arkansas and Indian country mostly. But every year there was at least a group or two from Missouri or even Iowa or Illinois. They were usually passing through Arkansas on their way to Texas. A lot of folks had felt a need to move on after Appomattox. The border country held too many memories, mostly bad ones and moving on seemed the best way to start fresh. A lot of men had gotten religion in the War, too. In leaving home, they looked for special guidance. And the Shiloh campmeeting had begun as a kind of anointing for those moving West and for those turning back to God.

Every year since the War's end, fewer were Westing, but the hunger for benediction and renewal never slacked. At the end of each summer, people came in their wagons with their families to camp for a week along Sleepy Creek and listen to the preaching and the singing, to find again something that couldn't be dug out of the farm or hung up on the clothes line, to let themselves go in the emotion the meeting brought. Some came in superstitious fear and appeasement of the vengeful force they called "god". And some came because the others were there and ripe for picking.

Reverend Poe's tent sat behind the preaching arbor in the trees. Josh walked the mare down the wide aisle between the log benches of the congregation.

"Preacher," he called out.

The tent flap flew open and the shirtsleeved evangelist offered his tent in a sweeping gesture.

"Get down, brother. It ain't fit to be out." Josh dismounted. "I'm prayin' it'll pass on over before the morning service. There's a lot of sinful souls a needin' salvation. You ain't been around here before, brother, air you?"

"I'm a Friend, Preacher."

"Ain't we all, brother, ain't we all. Set an' eat. Sister Woods just brought me a breakfast that'll bust two bellies."

He sat down and jammed a fork into an egg yolk. The orange-yellow contents oozed onto the plate.

"Love fried eggs. Women is a miracle, brother. To fix a breakfast like this in a drivin' storm."

"Preacher, did you hear the bells?"

"What bells?"

"The Shiloh death bells."

"No, can't says I did." He ran his tongue around his teeth. "You needin' a funeral preached in town? My fee's two dollars."

"We're not sure anyone's dead. The deaths are supposed to be out here in the camp. I've come to see."

"What's that you say?" Preacher Poe stuck a fingernail between his front teeth. "Who's dead out here?"

"The death note said Mary Neil, Jo Belle Walker, and Becka Beard."

The preacher stood up, overturning the table and

dumping the good breakfast onto the dirt. Still holding the fork and wearing his napkin he pushed past Josh and out the front of the tent. He paused a minute then headed around the log pews toward the women's tents. Shank followed, watching the hatless preacher throw down the useless fork and bull through brush and believers.

"They's down here together," he pointed toward a tent set away from the others as he slid standing down the hillside rocks.

By the time he reached the tent, Josh was at his side. They bent together to look inside. Nothing. The tent was empty except for little girl things scattered on the faded quilts—a hair ribbon, a broken comb, a rag doll, a pair of button shoes.

The preacher straightened. "Maybe they's gone to breakfast."

"Look," said Josh dropping to his knees and crawling inside.

He reached back into the corner and grasped a wadded nightdress. The white garment was wet and saturated with a dark substance. He lifted the rear flap over a muddy set of tracks. "They went out through here," he called back over his shoulder.

In the rain outside again, he handed the gown to the preacher. "My God, that's blood," the preacher said, turning the garment in his hands. Blood, pink and fading, ran with the rain through his fingers and onto his boots.

"What's happening?" a short solid woman with a parasol asked the men contemplating the dress. "My God! My God. That's my Mary's dress—"

Preacher Poe threw arms around the woman and held her to him. The disturbance drew others from the women's camp.

"Sister Leona, fetch the men."

Mrs. Neil struggled in his arms to see into the tent. "She ain't there, sister. Don't torment yourself a tryin' to see. What's your name, son?" he suddenly asked Josh.

"Joshua Shank."

The preacher's eyes glazed over with a biblical ecstasy. "They're over yonder across the Jordan, brother Joshua. Gird up the fighting men and lead them into the land of our enemy. Smite them. Smite them hip and thigh. Blood for blood. Eye for eye. Tooth for tooth. Kill the Amalekites, Joshua."

By this time, men were sliding down the slope to join the crowd gathering in the rain. "Look," shouted a boy pointing across the creek into the brush. Rain had washed the mud from something beneath the blackberry bushes. "It's a foot." The crowd surged toward the creek bank.

"Stop. Stop where you stand!" shouted Shank. "If you all crush about now, you'll ruin any clues the rain hasn't. You men, take your wives to their tents. The preacher'll tell you who's missing."

In the crowd Josh saw faces of men he knew. "Whiting, Trimble, LeFevre, come with me. Boy," he said to a youngster pulling up the tent flap, "my horse is at the preacher's tent. Ride to town. Tell Tom Bryan. 'It's true. Send for a marshall.' Then bring him back here. Don't talk to anybody else. Do you understand?" The boy nodded and ran up the hill.

"Trimble, get some help and try to keep people off this stuff around the tent. Whiting, LeFevre, let's see what's over there."

Joshua and his men waded into Sleepy Creek. Looking over his shoulder, he saw Trimble and another man guarding the tent. The preacher, still holding Mrs. Neil, was making his way up the rocky slope with the crowd behind him.

"Funny ain't it," said LeFevre. "Half hour ago folks couldn't think of anything but stayin' dry. Now they're walkin' around in the rain, and they don't even care."

There was no further talk as the three men walked up the muddy slope to where the foot had been seen. The body in the brush was that of a girl child, small and pale. The throat was cut out.

"Oh God," Whiting grabbed his mouth, walked a few feet away and leaned against a tree.

"Can you tell who it is, Josh?" asked LeFevre shifting the tobacco from his cheek.

"Jo Belle . . ." The words caught in Shank's throat. He cleared it. "It's Jo Belle Walker."

There is an evil killer loose in Shiloh. Quickly the terrified drive for revenge threatens to destroy not only the town but the nearby peaceful Cherokee nation. Although he is a Quaker, Joshua Shank is the only man strong enough to see the killer brought to justice without more blood being shed. Until suddenly the killer forces the man of peace into a death-stalk—the most savage encounter of Shank's entire life.

(Read the complete Bantam Book, A KILLER COMES TO SHILOH, by C. H. Haseloff, available June 15th wherever paperbacks are sold.)

Great stories of the Lone Star frontier

Elmer Kelton's
TALES OF

★

TEXAS

Elmer Kelton is one of the great storytellers of the American West with a special talent for capturing the fiercely independent spirit of his native Texas. Now, for the first time, Bantam Books has collected many of Elmer Kelton's exciting Western novels in a series, TALES OF TEXAS, to be published on a regular basis beginning in July, 1981.

Each of the TALES OF TEXAS is dramatically set in the authentic Texas past. These stories filled with the special courage and conflicts of the strong men and women who challenged a raw and mighty wilderness and fought to build a frontier legend —Texas.

CAPTAIN'S RANGERS

(*Available August 15th 1981*)

The Nueces Strip—a stretch of coastal prairie and desert wasteland lying between the two rivers that bordered Texas and Mexico. Long after the Mexican War this parched land remained a war zone, seared by hatred on both sides and torn by lawless raids of looting and burning. By the Spring of 1875 the Strip was ready to explode—for this was the year Captain McNelly and his Rangers were sent down from the North. Their mission— "clean up the Nueces Strip."

MASSACRE AT GOLIAD

(*Available September 15th 1981*)

In 1834 Thomas and Josh Bucalew came to he rugged new country that was Texas. The land that was soon to be ravaged by the battle of the Alamo, at the brutal massacre at Goliad and its bloody sequel, San Jacinto. Because of Thomas' hatred of Mexicans they separated, but the two brothers were re-united when the smoldering violence exploded into savage war.

(*Don't miss Elmer Kelton's TALES OF TEXAS, available wherever Bantam Books are sold.*)

LUKE SHORT
BEST-SELLING WESTERN WRITER

Luke Short's name on a book guarantees fast-action stories and colorful characters which mean slam-bang reading as in these Bantam editions:

"REACH FOR THE SKY!"

and you still won't find more excitement or more thrills than you get in Bantam's slam-bang, action-packed westerns! Here's a roundup of fast-reading stories by some of America's greatest western writers:

Bantam Book Catalog

Here's your up-to-the-minute listing of over 1,400 titles by your favorite authors.

This illustrated, large format catalog gives a description of each title. For your convenience, it is divided into categories in fiction and non-fiction——gothics, science fiction, westerns, mysteries, cookbooks, mysticism and occult, biographies, history, family living, health, psychology, art.

So don't delay——take advantage of this special opportunity to increase your reading pleasure.

Just send us your name and address and 50¢ (to help defray postage and handling costs).